VICIOUS PRINCE

ALSO BY LILI ST. GERMAIN

LILI ST. GERMAIN

USA TODAY BESTSELLING AUTHOR

San Francisco is going to burn if the coveted princess of California's criminal underworld isn't returned to her family in one piece ...

Avery Capulet is missing.

Taken by a madman. Kept in the dark.

She might not survive.

He'll use her body. Destroy her mind. All before he ever lays a hand on her.

Rome Montague is a drug dealer. A criminal. A thief.

And he needs the secrets Avery and her family are keeping – even if it means cutting them out of her pretty Capulet flesh.

Rome Montague is missing – but nobody will miss him.

Not that it matters.

After the things he's done to this girl?

He doesn't deserve to be found.

"These violent delights have violent ends …"

William Shakespeare, Romeo and Juliet

PROLOGUE

AVERY

Eight hours from now

n my family, we follow two religions.

Catholicism.

And an unbroken devotion to the Capulet family bloodline.

The Catholic side may seem more understandable to the uninitiated.

Be a good Catholic. Say your prayers. Go to Mass. Confess your sins.

But when you're raised a daughter of the most powerful man in California, ensconced in the heart blood of the Capulet lineage — loyalty to our family name is equal priority to God.

Capulets don't have a bible, but we do have

written rules. And unlike the bible, ours *are* written in blood.

Be a good Capulet. Obey your vows to the family. Go to family meetings. Ensure there are no sins against your own blood to confess. That last one being the most important.

Never sin against your family, because in our religion, there is no forgiveness. There is only loyalty, or death.

Sometimes, even when you are loyal, there is still death. All the protection of our father's money, our bodyguards and spies placed strategically around the city of San Francisco and beyond, can't save us.

Because hatred is stronger than any religion.

I wonder how much my captor hates me, as I strain in the dark to place his approaching footsteps.

I wonder how much of my blood he will spill before this is over.

I wonder which Capulet sins he intends to punish me for.

Because I wasn't afraid at first, see? No, when I woke up here, bound and gagged, I was bored. Annoyed. Like a customer in line at the bank, waiting for her turn, so I waited for my father to pay whatever ransom my captor demanded. Even as a young woman living in a city gripped by the terror of an active serial killer in its midst, picking off girls at the edges of society, I was not afraid. Arrogant? Absolutely. But worried that I might somehow become swept up in the bloodbath myself?

Hell no.

I'm a Capulet. People don't fuck with Capulets.

A ransom. A ransom. A ransom.

I imagine them making the call. Maybe they'll take my picture. Perhaps we'll Skype my father, because this is 2018, after all. I imagine him gathering crisp banknotes from one of our many vaults scattered across the city, stacks and stacks of green paper that will secure my release.

Even as I slowly came to in — *wherever it is that I am* — I was thinking about how this hiccup would affect my schedule, how brazen my kidnappers were, how my father would stick a goddamn blowtorch onto whoever did this and slowly, agonizingly, melt away their flesh as punishment.

Then it came rushing in, like ice water into my consciousness. *They shot my father.* A single gunshot that cracked everything apart. My father, in his tuxedo, dropping his whiskey on hard tiles, the glass exploding at his feet as blood blossomed across his white dress shirt.

His trajectory into the pool, the heavy splash of

his dead weight as five hundred people in ballgowns and designer suits screamed and scattered, nobody wanting to be gunshot victim number two.

My desire to jump into the water after my uncle, to help him save my dad. The hands that clamped around my arms hard enough to cause bruises, as my own personal security team whisked me away, to supposed safety, and straight into a trap.

Somebody shot my father just to take me. And they didn't fuck around. I saw where they shot him — right in the middle of his chest.

Is he even alive to know that I've been stolen away?

"My family will pay whatever ransom you want," I say to total darkness, over and over again. "Just tell them what you want. They'll give it to you." I don't even know if there is anyone with me. Whether somebody is watching me. I could be buried alive, or in somebody's attic, or in my own fucking house. I can't see. *I don't know.*

I've been in this fucking room for hours, and fear has begun to drip into my veins like a steady dose of poison leeching into my blood.

"Listen," I say, trying to be convincing, which is hard when I'm tied to a chair, my wrists and ankles secured with what feels like duct tape, a blindfold tied tight around my face. "Just tell me—"

What feels like a large, rough palm smacks me so hard, I feel my lip split, tasting fresh blood in my mouth. My mind struggles to catch up, to do something— but before I can think, before I can construct the perfect argument to *let me go*, my blindfold is ripped off, and in the same breath, shoved into my mouth. A makeshift gag that makes me retch. I swallow down the urge to vomit, the material in my mouth an invasion, an assault on my senses. I try to push it out with my tongue, but it doesn't budge.

Fuck. *Oh fuck oh fuck oh fuck.*

I forget about the gag as my eyes focus on the figure in front of me. He's tall, over six feet, dressed entirely in black, a black ski mask covering his face and neck. He's wearing plastic surgical gloves — to keep his DNA from getting on me, or in preparation to chop me into little pieces?

I wince as my captor places something cold on my bare thigh.

A knife.

My eyes go big and round as I watch him take that knife and press it into the flesh of my inner thigh. There is a major artery that runs through the thigh. If he hits it, I could bleed out in minutes.

Just hours ago, I was joking about how being married off was a fate worse than death. But I didn't really mean those words, because I'd do anything to stop the slow, methodical slice of the knife's teeth against my skin. I scream as my skin splits open, the knife impossibly sharp, my skin impossibly fragile.

There is so much blood.

I've seen plenty of blood spilled in my short life — a by-product of my family name — but I've never been so intimately acquainted with my own blood as it pulses from my body.

My captor dips a finger into my blood and brings it up to my chest. I'm folding forward, straining to see what he's doing to my thigh, and so he takes a fistful of my hair and yanks, making me sit straighter in the chair. I shiver as the air in the room turns colder, my exposed nipples tightening painfully, or perhaps it's me that is growing colder, as I swiftly lose blood.

Fingers paint letters between my breasts, a macabre action that reminds me of the crude paintings a small child would create with their hands and brightly colored paint. My faceless captor takes blood from my thigh wound several more times before he steps back, apparently satisfied, and it's only then that I can see what he's written on me.

. . .

*T*wo letters. **XO.**

I blink in confusion as I stare at the two letters, my chin against my chest as I try to make them say something — anything — else. Everybody knows the XO killer doesn't have any surviving victims. He's been terrorizing San Francisco for a decade, at least, the body count of his victims over a dozen. *And that's not including the ones who are never found.* He only leaves death in his wake, naked and scrubbed clean and with a neat calling card painted on his victims chests.

*X*o.

*I*t's so obvious now. This faceless man doesn't want a ransom. He wants my terror. My blood.

He wants my *life*.

This silent psycho circles behind me, hands in my hair again, and then lower, exploring my face, my neck, pinching a nipple hard enough to make me yelp. He pulls my hair, forcing my head back and to the side, at the perfect height to grind himself into my cheek. Under his black pants, he's as hard as the steel the knife is forged from. I start to cry. He's going to hurt me. *He's going to kill me.*

I raise my eyes to look at him again, in time to see him place the knife on the ground at his feet. My captor comes at me, crouching in front of me, placing his gloved hands on my knees and pushing them wider.

This is how I die.

Through my gag, I scream.

CHAPTER ONE

AVERY

Present Day

*J*oshua Grayson is sitting in my father's office, discussing a business deal as if today is any other day.

But it's not any other day. It's THE day. And everyone is acting like it's not.

Just moments ago, I watched him glide out of the Capulet Corporation's private elevator reserved only for family members. Perhaps that should have been my first warning that things were not going to go well. He winked at me as he passed me in the corridor, like he owned the place, casually unbuttoning his jacket as he scanned my father's office. Maybe he was wondering how he would decorate the place once his name was on the door.

Fuck that. When Daddy retires, this will be *my* office. I would have been content to study something arts-related, use my creativity, but you can't run a billion-dollar company with a degree in art history. I graduated summa cum laude from Stanford University with a degree in political science, not because I was interested in politics, but because it was the best subject for the Capulet heiress to study. I worked twice as hard as everyone else, graduated top of my class, and spent my free time working weekends and summers for my father, while my peers drank and fooled around and generally had fun.

And in the years since I graduated, I've been the first person here every morning, and the last to leave, apart from my father.

Not to mention, getting this corner office is kind of my birthright. I'm not giving up the best view in the building for any man, especially not Joshua Grayson.

There's nothing really wrong with him, and that's part of the problem. He's older than me, having just celebrated turning forty, but that's not a concern. Attractive in a smarmy sort of way, with his perfect white smile and his Ivy-League smirk, Joshua Grayson is exactly the kind of man I would choose to run a company — but not the kind of man I would choose to take to bed. Maybe it's the way he looks at me like I'm a child, all the more disturbing since he's known me my entire life. I'm all grown up now, but I know when he talks to me he still sees the shy teenage girl who had a habit of hiding behind her older, more confident sister.

"Avery," he nods, standing when I enter the room. "Happy birthday. Nice to see you before the big night."

"Thank you," I nod my hello, as bile burns in my throat.

"The weather's perfect for a rooftop soirée," he adds, trying to keep the conversation going. When he smiles, a deep dimple creases his right cheek. I'd like to stab my manicured nail into his dimple and wipe the smile right off his face. He has one of those deep voices that makes my chest hum when he speaks, but I can't say I enjoy listening to him.

"Perfect," I agree. I try so hard to be cordial, but it's already exhausting. I don't want to be talking to this guy. I don't want to be here. It's my twenty-fifth birthday, and I want to be having shots off some half-naked bartender's abs, not making small talk about the fucking weather with the guy my father wants me to marry.

"Well, I should let you two get on with it. I'll see you both tonight."

"Bye," I say, a little too loudly, a little too saccharine sweet. Josh is smart. He knows I can't stand him. So far, it hasn't swayed his quest to put a ring on my finger and a hefty percentage of Capulet stocks into his share portfolio.

I watch him button his jacket as he stands and leaves the office, making sure to brush past me with his elbow as he exits. His hands are big, but sophisticated, perfect for playing the piano. I wonder what he's like in bed, if he'd wrap that hand around my throat while he was inside me, or use it over my mouth to stifle a moan, and even though my cheeks pool with blood at the thought of fucking the guy who's just finished a business meeting with my father, something cold settles in my stomach.

Resignation. *Loss.*

It is something like dying, this process. I might be obedient and poised by day, nodding my head and smiling when it's appropriate, but in the dark my nightmares come to feed off me, hungry little vampires that sap me of every bit of strength and bravery that I possess. I bolt upright in the dead of night, when the only light is red numbers on my bedside table that tell me how many more hours until it's light again — the dark hours when all I can think about is how to stop the full-force collision my fate is careening toward.

I wait until the door swings shut before I turn to my father, letting out a breath. "Jesus fucking Christ, can you let me know next time I'm about to be ambushed by my stalker?"

"Avery!" My father says sharply. He's already drinking, a tumbler of whiskey in his hand as he turns from the window to address me.

"Happy birthday, dear daughter," I say in a silly voice, pretending to be him. "Why thank you, Daddy! I'm so glad I get to be paraded around San Francisco like a mail-order-bride on my birthday! How sweet of you to remember."

I flop down into the chair facing Daddy's large mahogany desk, the one that I'll be replacing with sleek glass and metal when it's my time to move in and let him retire somewhere exotic and remote. All of his old-school furniture makes the place feel stuffy, confined, even though this office takes up half the top floor of Capulet Corp.

"What was he doing here, anyway?"

My father looks at the ground. Panic floods me. "Daddy?" I raise my eyes in disbelief when he reaches into his pocket and pulls out a red Cartier box, setting it on the desk between us as if it's a bomb.

I snatch up the box, praying to the Jesus I just blasphemed ten seconds ago that there's a necklace or a pair of earrings, anything but—

An engagement ring. The diamond sticking out of the box is obscenely big. Princess cut, at least five carats, a diamond that could take somebody's eye out if you punched them while wearing it.

"What did you do," I mutter, my eyes fixed on the diamond.

"Avery —"

"What did you DO?!" I yell, closing the box and throwing it at the window. The glass is thick, bullet-proof, and not in the least bit bothered by my lazy overarm toss.

"Keep your voice down," my father hisses. "For God's sake, Avery, get your shit together. Don't you dare fuck this up."

"We said one more year."

"Things change."

"Dad," I say emphatically. "What about Will?"

"It's not like you can't see Will," he says casually. "You can love one man and be married to another. This is a business transaction, Avery. You and your children will still have everything your hearts desire."

I swallow a sob. "I don't want to have Joshua Grayson's children," I say forcefully. "Children should come from love, not obligation."

"You and your sister came from obligation," he says. "And your mother and I loved you just the same."

"What about my brother?" I ask. "Did he come from obligation? Or did you finally love Mom after fifteen years together?"

I think of the baby brother nestled in the crook of my mother's arm as family filed past their open — shared — coffin. How I reached out to touch the baby's cheek, even though I'd been forbidden from doing so on the way to the funeral home. How cold he was, the stillborn son of Augustus Capulet, the longed-for male heir who died during childbirth and took my mother along with him, into that endless night.

Rage sparks in my father's dark eyes. "Don't speak ill of the dead." A beat. "I loved your mother *very* much."

When my father gets angry, it's like all the air whooshes out of a room. My empty lungs try to draw in a breath, and the room starts to spin. I almost feel guilt for bringing up Mom, and the baby my father talked her into having. But then I think of the way he's marrying me off to essentially the highest bidder, despite my protests, despite his promises that there was more time, and the tiny grain of guilt disappears.

My heart starts to beat faster. My clothes are suddenly too tight, the room's walls pressing in on all sides. My vision narrows. My palms grow damp with sweat. And through all of this, I'm acutely aware that Josh is probably listening outside.

"Breathe," my father snaps. Daddy calls me petulant and spoiled when I have a panic attack. It's something I try to make sure I never do in front of him. In front of anybody.

"I don't want this," I gasp.

"Well, we don't always get what we want," he replies flatly, rounding his desk, leaning against the edge with crossed arms as he watches me hyperventilate.

The office doors hiss open. I jerk in fright, wiping at my face. As if this couldn't get any more humiliating, Josh has come back into the office to — what?

Retrieve the ring I unceremoniously threw and force it onto my finger?

"What'd I miss?" A light-hearted male voice interjects the tense silence.

I sit up in my seat, softening as some of the panic leaves me. "Uncle Enzo," I say. I watch as my father's younger brother spots the Cartier box on the floor, frowns, and bends to pick it up. He tosses it up in the air like a baseball, catching it and then throwing it at me. I put my hands out to catch it just before the hard edge of the box hits me square in the face.

"That could have left a bruise," I snap, slamming the box down on the desk.

Enzo grins, holding his arms out. "It's my favorite niece's birthday," he says, holding his hand out to me. I shake my head, refusing to reciprocate.

"What's wrong?" Enzo asks, switching his attention to the Cartier box. "Did that little punk not get you a big enough ring?" He opens the box and blinks, whistling. "Jesus, Mary and Joseph. Don't show your Aunt Eliza this. She'll throw up from envy when she sees this rock."

I cross my arms, smiling bitchily. "She can have it."

Enzo sighs. "You'd better fill me in, Augie." Enzo

is the only one my father allows to call him Augie. Everyone else calls him by his full name, Augustus.

"Yeah, Augie," I add, my voice like liquid acid. "You'd better fill Enzo in."

Daddy glares at me as he addresses his younger brother. "Avery's angry that I've decided to bring up the engagement."

"Ahh," Enzo nods. "That."

"Just tell me why," I insist. "Tell me why it has to be him." I jerk my thumb toward the door, and beyond, to the stranger whose engagement ring I'll be wearing in about six hours. "Tell me why it can't be the man I'm *actually* in love with."

"Sweetheart—"

"Do not *sweetheart* me," I cut in. "I did everything you said. I didn't even look at a boy unless he met your predetermined checkboxes. Will's family has money, they are respected, they are healthy—"

"Will's father is a goddamn Hollywood action hero," Daddy yells, pounding his desk for effect. "You're not marrying his son and making a mockery of the Capulet name. We might be in California, my darling daughter, but this isn't a *fucking* reality show."

I just stare.

My father is up now, pacing the well-worn length of carpet behind his desk.

"He's right," my uncle says. "The Hewitt's are risky, at best."

"You led me to believe Will was a possibility," I argue. "You were never going to even *consider* him, were you?"

Both of their faces say it all.

"Will isn't a celebrity. He doesn't give interviews. He doesn't even live in Hollywood! Remember? He moved away from his family and emancipated himself just so he could be closer to me."

Silence.

"You lied to me, you fucking *bastard*."

Daddy shakes his head, squeezing his tumbler so tight I hope it shatters.

"What do you want, Avery?" he spits. "A flow chart? A pros and cons list? *A fucking Venn diagram*?"

"It wouldn't hurt," I reply. "I mean, if you can spare five minutes to explain how you've chosen how my life unfolds, I'm all ears. And stop fucking swearing at me."

"Five minutes," he mutters. "We've been explaining this to you for almost ten years, Avery. Jesus Christ, it's the day of your inauguration."

"I won't have his children," I protest. "I won't have any children."

"No problem," my father says.

"No problem?" I echo. I look at my uncle, who won't meet my gaze. "What'd you do, harvest my eggs?" I half-joke.

Neither of them says anything.

"Holy fucking shit." My stomach drops. I feel like I've been electrocuted. I'm stunned. I think back to when it could have happened. "My appendectomy," I breathe. "After Adeline died."

"On the bright side, you still have a perfectly good appendix," Enzo interjects. "We just thought it best to preserve the only chance of continuing the bloodline in case—"

"— In case I drowned myself, too?" I think of my sister, floating facedown in our pool, her hair spread out in the water, creating a dark halo around her. She'd already been dead for hours by the time I stumbled across her body.

"We can use a gestational carrier, if you prefer," Enzo says, sidestepping the mention of my dead sister — the one who was meant to take on all of this instead of me. "The embryos are already on ice, ready to go. We all know how important your career is to you."

My father gives him a sharp look. I feel hot tears stab at my eyes as I put a hand to my stomach. They haven't just taken my eggs. They've created embryos with them?

"What the actual *fuck?!*" I demand.

"You should have told her," Enzo says tersely.

My father throws his hands up in response.

"Where?" I ask. My head is swimming. "When? Who is the father?"

Enzo looks at me like I'm an idiot, but then I see something flash in his eyes. *Guilt.* "Have you not been listening to anything?" He turns to my father, a deep frown etched between his eyebrows. "I told you to tell her," he mutters, and his voice wavers a little, thick with regret. It's almost as if he's the one who has been betrayed.

Enzo focuses on me again. "Joshua Grayson's sperm. Your eggs. Thirteen embryos that are richer than sin the moment they become your children."

I choke so hard, I almost vomit. "*Thirteen?*"

Enzo looks bereft. "Obviously you don't have to use all of them."

"Or *any* of them," I snap.

"Both of you, *shut up*," my father says. "Avery, we will talk about this when the time is right. You're not even engaged yet."

"Daddy—" I interrupt.

"You're a little old to be using that word," he says, all trace of paternal concern gone, replaced by irritation. I bristle.

"Oh, fuck you," I spit. "Why all the trouble with the egg extraction, huh? Hell, you could've saved yourself the trouble and passed me off to Joshua at Adeline's funeral. Let him fuck your sixteen-year-old daughter in the back of the church and knock her up while you buried her sister? Or maybe you should have just locked me in a room and let him breed me like a fucking animal. I mean really, what's the goddamn difference, *Augie*?"

My father's open palm smacks into my cheek before I even see him move. The side of my face hums angrily, but the pain doesn't bother me. It steels me. I'll do what I'm told, but it doesn't mean I won't make it a living hell for everyone concerned.

Enzo quickly steps between us, motioning for my father to back up. Ever the concerned uncle, he brushes his knuckles against my cheekbone, his touch cool against the blood-red rage that has risen in my cheeks.

"This is not the time, Avery," he murmurs, raising his eyebrows in a silent warning as he gazes down at me. Enzo has a way of looking at me that makes all of my emotion pour out. It's always been this way between us. While Daddy worked and grieved in his office after everyone else was dead and gone, it was Enzo who became my parent.

"That's the problem, Enzo," I say bitterly, pushing him away. "Time has run out."

Daddy refills his whiskey. Enzo holds his hand up, signaling to pour one more. I seethe as I switch my attention between the two men who just delivered my death sentence.

I snatch Enzo's whiskey before he can take it from my father's outstretched hand, and pour it down my throat in one gulp. It burns. I like it. I drop the glass at my feet, where it bounces harmlessly on the thick carpet, before repeating the same action with my father's full glass. More burn. More warmth, spreading through my veins, sating my anxious limbs. I don't drop the second glass, though. I draw my arm back and throw it as hard as I can, narrowly missing my father and Enzo and hitting the window my father stands in front of. The whiskey tumbler explodes loudly, showering the expensive carpet with even more shards of expensive crystal.

My father smiles slowly, but there is a darkness behind the gesture, a chilling promise of what is to come. "There's my girl."

"Your girl for another—" I look down at my delicate gold watch, the one my mother left me in her will, "—six hours and thirty-five minutes."

It's time to go. I snatch up the Cartier box, straightening my skirt, and turn on my Louboutin heel, rolling my eyes as I walk away.

"You'll always be my little girl," he calls out. "No matter how old you are."

"You could have warned me," I throw over my shoulder, making a beeline for the heavy mahogany doors of what will soon be my office in our opulent tower of lies.

"I did it this way for your own good," he replies, always the one to have the last word.

I smack my palm against the door, my wrist throbbing from the force I use. The door concedes, flying open to reveal the man I've been trying to avoid for the past decade, the exhausting presence, my friendly stalker, always around my father's office, the hotel, our house, giving me lingering glances and getting in my personal space at every opportunity.

I set my face to a stony blankness, fresh anger a geyser inside my chest, waiting to explode and burn everyone it touches.

Joshua. He's hovering near the elevator. *Great.*

He's probably been listening to the entire thing. The entire diatribe about how he only wants my money.

I need my mother. I miss my sister. Right now, in this moment, I fucking loathe Adeline and the way she left me to all of this. My get-out-of-Verona-free card. Tonight should be her night, the prodigal Capulet daughter, the first-born jewel in the family crown; but she obviously saw the same cold fate written in Joshua Grayson's blue-grey eyes that is now in front of me, and decided death was preferable to a life lived only for others.

"I gather you heard that?" I ask Joshua. Fuck niceties.

He smiles. "Some."

I toss the Cartier box at him. "I believe this belongs to you."

"For six hours and thirty-five minutes," Joshua Grayson smirks, echoing my words. He glances at his watch. "Make that six hours and thirty-four minutes."

"I guess time doesn't fly when you're not having fun," I retort. "Did you know about all of this?"

"If you're talking about the embryos, yes. I've known since your surgery."

I snort. "Unbelievable."

"Avery—"

"I was a *child*," I cut in. A child who had just lost

her sister, and just before that, her mother, and her baby brother."

"Exactly," Joshua says smoothly. "Your father and Enzo were worried about the family bloodline continuing after such losses. Don't forget, I was not a decision-maker in that process. I was told, same as you've just been told."

I blink, the alcohol hitting me, making me dizzy for a second. I wait for Joshua to fill in the silence, but he doesn't. Awkward silences are his specialty.

"I get it," Joshua finally breaks the silence, brushing imaginary lint from my shoulder. "This marriage is a choice for me. It's not for you."

There are no choices for me.

"I won't make any of this easy," I vow, leaning away from him.

"Avery, I've known you your whole life," Joshua says, smiling fondly, sending shivers of dread up my spine. "You don't make anything easy."

"Ugh," I make a gagging sound. "I have to go."

"Where?"

For an eternal swim. Part of me wants to drown myself like my sister did, just to spite him.

"Why?" I say slowly. "You want to come?"

"I always want to come when you're concerned."

Did he really just say that? He's smirking. Of course he just said that.

"I'm going to the family mausoleum," I clarify. "You still feel like you want to come?"

His smirk disappears.

"That's what I thought," I continue. "I'm going to confession, and then to pay my respects to my sister. Remember her?"

"You go to confession a lot," Joshua says, dodging my jibe. He grabs my elbow as I make a move to walk away. I look at his hand like it's a dirty cockroach, before meeting his gaze. "Maybe I have a lot of things to confess," I say smoothly.

"You won't have to visit your little boyfriend in a dirty old graveyard once we're married," he says, squeezing my arm tighter. "Hell, I'll build you both your own wing when you move in to my house. You'll need somebody to spend all those lonely nights with while I'm here, working."

"How generous of you," I say. "Make sure it's far, far away from wherever you'll be fucking *your* mistress."

He tips his head back and laughs, tugging me into him suddenly and whispering in my ear. "Avery, there's only one woman I'll be fucking. My *wife*."

I shove him forcefully, finally breaking free of his

grip. "Don't touch me again," I warn him, backing away. "I'm not yours yet, Joshua."

"Happy birthday," he calls down the hallway, as I retreat. "Next year I'll arrange a proper celebration. Maybe we'll have our wedding ceremony on your twenty-sixth birthday. Hell, maybe you'll already be knocked up with my baby by then. Wait, sorry. *Our* baby."

He's lucky he's not within striking distance when he says that.

CHAPTER TWO

AVERY

*J*have my driver take me home, through city traffic and up to Verona, where we have to pass through two security checkpoints to make it onto the gated part inside the gated community where all the billionaires park their helicopters and store their supermodel wives.

I run through the foyer, across marble floors, taking the sweeping mahogany staircase two steps at a time. In my bedroom, I strip as fast as I can, my outfit suffocating me. I throw my clothes in the corner, vowing to burn them after Joshua touched me while I was wearing them. I stand in the middle of my walk-in closet, hands on my hips, wearing only my bra and panties as I scan racks upon racks of clothes for an appropriate outfit to wear to confession.

"Where have you been?" A voice comes from the bathroom attached to the other end of the walk-in-wardrobe. I don't bother covering up. You'd see more of me in a bikini.

"Out," I reply, not looking at my cousin as he saunters into the closet that separates our bedrooms.

"In that?" Nathan asks, smoking a joint as he leans against the doorframe, dressed in a black shirt and jeans. "I know you don't get access to your trust fund until tonight, but are you really so hard up that you're hooking on a Tuesday afternoon?"

I give him daggers. "Are you really so disinter-ested in working for our family's company that you're getting stoned on a Tuesday afternoon?" I take three steps toward him, plucking the joint out of his fingers and placing it between my lips, sucking deeply. The smoke snakes into my lungs, and I hold it there as long as I can before puffing it out. I place the joint back in his hand, staring into eyes that match mine. We both have these eyes that aren't brown, or gold, or hazel, but a mixture of all three. We could be siblings, we look so similar — or cousins — which we are, but also, we aren't. Nathan is adopted. He's the oldest Capulet in our generation, two years older than me, but when you don't have Capulet blood like the rest of us, you don't get to sit on the throne and bark orders.

"You smell like a liquor store," Nathan says. "Bad day?"

I select a bright red Tom Ford dress and hold it against my body, before tossing it aside. I need black. Today is a day of mourning and loss, not vibrancy and celebration. I look at my bright red nails, suddenly annoyed that I hadn't thought to paint them gloss black for today.

"Bad day," I agree, snatching a black A-line dress from a hanger and dragging it over my head. I stand in front of the floor-to-ceiling mirror in the middle of the closet, pulling the dress into place over my hips.

Nathan is at my back before I need to ask, holding the joint between his teeth, scooping my long, dark waves off my back and draping them over my shoulder so he can get to the zipper. He looks at me in the mirror, raising his eyebrows in question. I nod, and he zips the dress up at the back.

"You look like you're going to a funeral," Nathan remarks. "*Are* you going to a funeral?"

I smooth down my hair, heading to the bathroom in search of black eyeliner. "Kind of," I say, locating my eyeliner pencil and bringing it up to my face. "Did you know our fathers had my eggs harvested when I was sixteen years old and used them to make and freeze embryos?"

Nathan's mouth opens in surprise, and the joint falls to the ground. "What?"

"With Joshua Grayson's sperm." I bend over, picking up the joint and handing it back to him.

Nathan's hands clench at his sides. "I'm going to fucking kill them," he rages.

"Let's kill them later," I say quickly, not wanting Nathan to get too caught up in his revenge fantasy. "I have to go and break up with Will."

Nathan scrubs his palm across his chin, clearly agitated by my news.

"I think I smoked too much," he says, looking between the joint and me. "You're saying some really fucked up shit."

I sigh loudly, taking the joint from him and placing it between my lips again with an air of finality. He might be too stoned, but I'm not stoned enough. Time to balance things out.

"Nobody wears that much eye makeup to a funeral," Nathan says, watching me layer black crayon under my eyes like I'm about to play Cleopatra in a high school play. "Not even a hooker."

I open my mouth to correct him, but then I stop. He's right. I might be incredibly high-class, but at the end of the day, my pimp Daddy did just sell me to Joshua Grayson.

"This hooker does," I mutter, throwing the eyeliner pencil down onto the bathroom counter and handing him back the joint. "Don't come to my birthday party high," I warn Nathan, pointing a finger at his face to really drive it home.

"I gotta go." I go to kiss him on the cheek, and he stops me.

"Were you serious? Did they really do that to you?"

I nod. "Apparently. On the bright side, I still have a fully functional appendix."

Why am I not upset? Why aren't I throwing myself on my bed, kicking and screaming and hugging the sheets to me and weeping until my eyes feel like they're going to bleed?

"Avery," Nathan says slowly. "I'm sorry. I didn't know."

"Don't be sorry," I reply, squeezing his hand for a moment. "You didn't do anything."

"I would have done something if I'd known," he says.

I nod, smiling sadly. "I know you would."

Nathan frowns. "Are you going to live with him, then?"

I shrug. "No. Yes. I don't know. What am I going to do without you?"

My eyes linger on the door at the other end of the closet. I don't sleep well, have never slept well, so whenever Nathan is around he's usually rudely awoken by me hopping into whichever bed he's crashed out in. He stays on his side and I on mine, but hearing his steady, even breaths as he sleeps stops the worst of my nightmares from seeping in.

And now I'll be sleeping with a strange man I've never even been alone with.

Nathan breaks the silence. "I'll be around, Aves, just like always. It's us against the world, remember?"

I nod, suddenly feeling very small, my shoulders curving forward and down, heavy with my defeat. I knew I'd have to give up Will. I didn't realize I'd be giving up the only person who's kept me sane these past years since Adeline died. "You're my best friend in the world," I say in a small voice. "You're all I have." I sound like a little girl when I say it. Nathan smiles, but there's emotion behind the gesture, a heaviness that feels like grief. He doesn't reply. He just keeps looking sad. If sadness were fire, I think forlornly, our grief would burn this house down, just like the one next door, the one that used to belong to a family just like ours.

A sense of impending doom threads around my lungs and pulls tight as my driver takes us closer and closer to the dead center of town; the old farmland outside of the city that used to contain vegetables underneath it's topsoil, not decomposing bodies.

Holy Cross Cemetery is probably the largest and the most grand of the seven cemeteries that are dotted through Colma, the place that houses one and a half million dead people who used to live and work and love in San Francisco City at one time or another. It's also where my mother and my sister are interred, their bodies secure in the Capulet family mausoleum. I visit them every week. My father hates me coming here, and so I probably come here even more just to spite him.

My driver drops me off at the front of the imposing chapel that sits on Holy Cross Cemetery

Grounds. When I enter through the large wooden doors, the sounds of a children's choir flood out. They must be practicing, I think. It's a school day — where did these kids come from? There isn't a school nearby. The dead don't need to learn how to read. I stand there for a moment, letting their high-pitched little voices wash over me. The sound is quite beautiful, and at the same time, completely haunting.

It is eerie walking up the long corridor between the church pews as these small children fill the huge room with their voices. They sound like angels. And I all I can think about is death. The death of freedom. The death of hope.

When I get to the confession box, it is empty. A welcome reality. I don't want to wait around for this, and I definitely don't want to confess later, not after what I'm about to do.

Better to get my sins out before I commit more.

I close the little door behind me and open the screen that separates me and the priest. He makes a noise motioning that he is there ready to listen. I take a deep breath, "Bless me, Father, for I have sinned. It's been one week since my last confession. Since then I have committed mortal sin."

"Go on."

"Well," I say. "There are a few."

"God absolves all of his children who repent," the priest says. "Tell me, what would you like to share today?"

"I planned to commit adultery."

The priest clears his throat. "Did you go through with your plan?"

"No," I reply. "I'm not married yet. I'm not even engaged."

"Go on."

"I'm thinking about killing my unborn children. Isn't that a mortal sin?"

"Are you pregnant?"

My hand goes to my belly again, before I even notice. "No." *Not yet.*

"Then there is no mortal sin."

"I lied. I lied a lot."

"Yes, child. God will forgive you all your sins. Is there anything else?"

I lean back, letting my head rest against the back of the confessional booth. "I thought about murdering somebody this afternoon." Several people, if we're to be honest. Starting with Joshua.

"Did you actually murder somebody?" the priest asks.

"No, of course not. That would be terrible."

"Is there anything else you would like to confess?"

"I had pre-marital sex in my family's mausoleum last week after confession. I liked it a lot."

A stunned pause. "Anything else?"

"No. I think that about covers it for now."

"Fine," he says, his voice dripping with disapproval. "I absolve you of your sin. Do ten Hail Marys and ten Our Fathers, and next time, Avery, get a room. The Lord knows you have enough."

I grin as I exit the confessional booth. Maybe I *should* get a room, but I won't. It's better this way, hiding amongst the dead.

The children have stopped singing. The church is suddenly quiet. The space is cavernous, and when I walk back outside, my high heels echo in the large space like machine gun fire. I make it outside, and then I take my time walking through the grounds of Holy Cross toward the graves. The oldest ones are first. Individual plots, some with headstones, some unmarked.

I remember my father telling me about how hundreds of thousands of bodies were buried here in mass graves after the real estate in the city became too valuable to waste on graveyards, and San Francisco banned any new burials in the city limits. I think of how many dead people I'm walking over as I make my way to possibly the only other living person in this entire three-hundred-acre cemetery.

The Capulet mausoleum, a giant marble monolith that houses the dead members of my family, is locked. It's always locked, but that's not a problem. I have a key.

I unlock the heavy, gold-plated doors, pushing them open with an eerie creak. I like to think it's not the smell of death that greets me, but who am I kidding, what else could it be? A damp, musty smell invades my nostrils mixed with something sharper, something like formaldehyde.

I close the doors behind me. It's really fucking dark in here, as dark as I imagine hell would be if the devil extinguished all the flames.

I use my iPhone torch to illuminate the room. It's nothing elaborate really, not when you're used to living in mansions like mine. But I suppose for a dead person, it is quite grand. It's one long rectangular room with spaces built in on three walls to house the dead.

We inter our dead here. We don't cremate them.

We're Catholic, and we're filthy fucking rich. We can easily afford the real estate for an entire coffin. Or twenty. I've lost count of how many people are buried here.

But I suppose they're not really buried.

They're sealed into the walls.

"Hey." Normally a voice in a space reserved for the dead would spook somebody, but I've been expecting this one. A lighter sparks to life, lighting a candle.

"Hey, yourself," I say, kicking off my shoes, feeling the cold of the old marble tiles on the floor as I make my way toward the voice.

"I thought you were never going to get here," he says.

"Well, I'm glad you waited for me. I had a lot of things to confess."

Another candle is lit, and this time, I reach my hand out for it. We've done this a thousand times before. We have our whole ritual down pat now. But today ... today will be different. Today will be final.

Something cold settles in my chest as I think of the conversation that I had with my father and my uncle about how differently I thought tonight was going to turn out, but how I'm not surprised at all by the turn of events.

"Happy birthday, baby," Will says. His face is illuminated by the candle he holds, his perpetually messy dirty blond hair hanging in his eyes..

"Did you just wake up?" I ask, running my fingers through his hair. He jerks his head back, using his free hand to mess it up again. "It takes hours of my time to get this happening," he smirks. "But I'm pretty sure you didn't come here for hairstyling tips."

All of a sudden, my boyfriend — the one I'm not allowed to marry — pulls me toward him, wraps me in a giant bear hug, almost lighting my hair on fire.

"Hey. Whoa," I say, getting my balance, holding my candle as far away as my outstretched arm can. "We're going to burn this place down if we're not careful," I say. Will ignores my concerns. He smiles as he bends down to kiss me, the knuckles of his free hand tipping my chin up, his tongue meeting mine. I let out a little sigh as the tension in my body melts a fraction, chased away by the tongue-sex we're having. Will's kiss is long and deep, and it takes my breath away. It distracts me for a few seconds from everything that's about to happen, and for that, I am grateful.

"You're quiet," he says, pulling away, taking my candle from me, placing both candles on the altar at the end of the room. "Pussycat got your tongue?"

"I've got a lot going on in this head," I say, looking at the floor.

"Well," he says, wrapping a hand around my waist and pulling me towards him again, "let's see if we can get rid of some of those thoughts for a while. Huh?"

I nod, closing my eyes as he presses his lips to my forehead, then my cheek, and finally, over my mouth. "Yeah," I breathe between kisses. "I'd like that."

He palms my breasts through the black fabric of my dress, then tugs. The dress is tight, but the straps are wide enough that he manages to shove them down my shoulders, letting my tits spill out of the top. My nipples stiffen against the cold, and I groan when he sucks my right nipple into his mouth and bites ever-so-gently, repeating the action on the left one.

He grins, his blue eyes full of desire. "Lift up your dress."

A thrill of lust pulses through my body and settles in my core, a steady throb that demands attention. I take the hem of my dress and drag it up my thighs, slowly, savoring the way Will watches me, as if he's a lion and I'm the prey he's going to sink his teeth into. His hands go to my panties, pulling them down my thighs, unhooking them from my feet, holding them up to his mouth.

"Jesus *fuck*," he mutters into my soaked panties,

and somehow the words sound so much worse because of where we are. I watch, mesmerized, as he sucks on the fabric that was against my pussy just seconds ago. He shoves them in his pocket; they belong to him, now. My heart sinks as I realize this is probably the last time he's going to steal my panties from me.

Will unbuttons his pants with one hand, releasing his cock. It bounces out, hard and thick and pointed straight at me.

"Come here," he says, his voice strangled. He pumps his cock, a bead of precum appearing on the tip. I lick my lips, watching as he swipes the tip with his thumb and brings it up to my mouth.

"Suck," he murmurs.

I take his thumb into my mouth, the salty taste of him a tease of what's to come. I suck hard enough to make him groan. "Avery, you're fucking *killing* me."

No, but I'm about to. I release his thumb from my mouth with a wet pop, sinking to my knees. The marble floors are hard and cold, but I barely feel them as I wrap my fingers around Will and guide him into my hungry mouth. I moan around him as he threads his fingers into my hair and pulls, bottoming out when he hits the back of my throat.

I gag, my eyes watering as Will pulls out of my

mouth, strings of saliva glistening like tiny webs between his cock and my lips. I take a shuddering breath before he pushes into my mouth again, the back of my head braced against the side of the altar as Will fucks my face. I wrap my hands around the back of Will's knees to hold myself steady, my clit throbbing, begging for stimulation.

My father's words come back to haunt me as I shiver in the cold darkness: *You can be married to one man and in love with another.* If there's one thing I know about Will, it's that he's too proud to be somebody's dirty secret. The only reason he's my dirty secret now is because I've promised him things in the dark that I'll never be able to give him in the light of day.

Things he deserves. A wife who loves him. Babies, made with love, in a bed in a house, not made in a fucking cemetery or during a secret tryst. Emotion threatens to consume me, to turn my lustful pants into full-on sobs, but I push my tears down. If he sees me losing my mind, the gig is up. Not yet. *We need more time.*

"Fuck me," I pant when he pulls out of my mouth.

"I thought you'd never ask," Will deadpans, letting go of my hair and putting his hands under my shoulders, yanking me to my feet. His cock is a rod of molten steel pressed between us as he molds his hips to mine. He fuses my mouth with his, his body covering mine, and he tastes so fucking good, I can't bear it.

Am I ever going to kiss him again?

He fumbles in his pocket, producing a foil packet that he rips open with his teeth. I watch as he rolls the condom on, pressing my thighs together to try and ease the throb between them a little, when I grab Will's wrist.

"No condom," I blurt out. "Just us."

Will laughs. "Don't joke."

His smile disappears as he sees I'm serious. I take my hand from his wrist and start to pull the condom from his cock, breathing nervously. I've never had sex without protection before. It was something drilled into my head when I was twelve years old, the day I got my first period. My father sat me down and explained the birds and the bees — in all it's clinical, anatomically correct, sometimes horrifying detail for a child to understand.

I remember sitting on my hands in the chair across his desk, my stomach cramping painfully from my first ever bleed, wishing my mother were alive to soften the blow of becoming a woman. I'll never forget Daddy sliding a carton of condoms across the table as he told me he knew he couldn't stop me from having sex — but if I ever came home pregnant, I would have to have surgery to get rid of the baby.

He told me all about *that*, too.

Girls in our family who get pregnant before they're supposed to, or to boys they're not going to marry, get abortions and are never allowed to leave the house again.

Will knows this. He got the same talk from my father when we started dating. We hadn't even held hands and my father was threatening to cut his dick off if he ever put it in me without a rubber firmly wrapped around it.

There really are no boundaries the men in my family won't cross to keep decorum.

Will and I have done just about everything. He's a filthy boy, and I'm a dirty girl. But we've never, ever, not even for a second, been skin on skin like that. This, despite the fact that I have an IUD fitted that prevents pregnancy. But nothing is one hundred percent. Nothing is guaranteed. And we've just always been overly cautious.

Until now. I just want to feel him inside me, with nothing to separate us. The thought of him coming inside me makes my whole body flush with anticipation, with rebellious lust. And he's angry. He'll be rough. *Good.*

Before I can get the condom all the way off, Will grabs my wrist, moving my hand away from him. I reach for him again and he smacks my hand away. The next thing I know, his fingers are sliding along my drenched pussy, and then he's pushing them inside, three fingers, all the way to the knuckle. I gasp at the unexpected penetration, my hands clutching at the edge of the altar, a moan escaping my lips. A moment later he presses his thumb against my clit and starts to rub it, rough and insistent, as he fucks me with his hand.

"Wider," he says, kicking the inside of my foot with his, forcing my legs farther apart so he can go deeper.

"Will—"

"No talking," he cuts me off, pumping his fingers harder. I can hear how wet I am, because my arousal makes an audible noise every time he moves his fingers inside me. "There are only two reasons you would let me fuck you bare," he continues, his thumb so insistent against my clit that I'm almost coming on his hand. I'm struggling to catch up. Will's an excellent lover, but he's not usually like *this*.

"Reason one," he grinds out. "Your father finally decided to let you marry my dumb ass."

"Will, please," I beg. I'm not even sure what I'm begging for — him to let me talk, or let me have my orgasm, or for him to fuck me?

"I said. No. *Talking.*" He wraps one hand around my throat and squeezes, not hard enough to scare me, but enough to reduce my air supply to the bare minimum. Will keeps thrusting into me with his fingers, bringing me close to breaking point. I pant against his chokehold, taking tiny sips of air as my head begins to spin, my hips mimicking his movements as my body cries for release.

"Reason two," he continues, anger rolling off him in waves. "Your father finally decided to make you marry that *fucking* pedophile who's been following you around since you were a kid."

His eyes tell me he already knows the answer. He swallows with difficulty, looking up at the ceiling for a moment. His fingers loosen around my throat, his other hand gone from between my thighs. "You're *my* girl," he says, his voice thick with emotion. When he looks back at me, his hazel eyes are shining. "I'm not letting him do this to us, Aves."

I think about the embryos Enzo told me about. How, if I don't follow my father's plans, I have absolutely no doubt my family will continue in my absence. They'll use my own unborn children as ammunition against me, against the boy I love. And it's not just that. I fear what my father will do to Will if he sees him as a threat to his grand plans.

My father has had people killed for less. Much, much less. I've loved Will since I was seventeen years old. And the last thing I want to do is be the reason he ends up dead in a hit-and-run, or from a mysterious overdose, or just plain disappears, never to be seen again.

My cousin Ty's girlfriend disappeared three years ago, after he got careless and she got knocked up. They found her in Mexico, in a poppy field. Or, they found pieces of her, buried amongst the flower beds. My cousin was never the same after that. He never suspected his own family, but I did. I know what the Capulets are capable of doing in the name of blood.

"I have to," I whimper. "I'm sorry."

"You will be," Will snaps. "Take your dress off."

I unzip my dress and push it down over my hips, letting it pool on the floor like a dark puddle around my feet. I'm completely naked now, my nipples so hard they ache, my body desperately craving to be filled.

Will dips his head, pressing his forehead against

mine as he reaches between us. He's still hard, the head of his cock purple with need.

"Wrap your legs around me," Will murmurs, ripping the condom off and dropping it on the floor. He lets go of my throat and uses both of his hands to grab my ass, lifting me in the air. My pussy rubs against his cock as he carries me three steps, slamming me against the mausoleum wall. Holding me against the wall with one hand under my ass and the weight of his body to pin me still, he uses his other hand to guide himself to my entrance. I don't think I've ever been so naked, so desperate, so fucking turned on.

"I'm not letting him take you away from me," Will says through gritted teeth, pushing into me. It's different like this, skin on skin. It's never felt this good before.

"I'm *sorry*," I say again, screaming as he seats himself in one violent thrust.

Will pulls back, gripping my chin with his thumb and forefinger, his skin hot, the room cold. "Avery," he says, and then something clicks for him. He sees it in my face. He knows I'm not going to fight for him, at least not in the way he wants me to. *He knows I'm going to marry Joshua.* And the rage inside him, when he realizes this, needs somewhere to go.

I open my mouth to explain, but Will clamps a hand over my mouth. His gaze is like fire, and in that moment, it's like he sees everything I've ever kept from him in one devastating flash. I hear his teeth grind together, his jaw straining as he searches for my eyes. Is he looking for hope? For something to redeem me?

Whatever it is he's looking for, he obviously doesn't find it. He takes his hand away from my mouth slowly, his intent clear: *Don't speak.*

So I don't. I stay silent, watching him, both of us still breathing heavily, me still impaled on his cock, wet and needy and trying desperately to stop my hips from the shallow thrusts they seem to be doing of their own accord, as my body tries to draw him deeper. Even physically, I feel like I'm losing him.

"Will," I sob.

His expression turns to pure rage, but I'm not afraid. Not when he takes my wrists in his hands and pulls them down by my sides. He makes a low sound in his throat, almost a growl, as he smashes my wrists against the hard marble wall. It hurts, shock waves of pain lancing from my wrists through my body. I choke on a moan as Will's fingers return to my throat and squeeze again.

"I love you," Will says, choking me as he rears

back, almost pulling out of me. "But I fucking *hate* you, Avery."

He slams into me on the word *hate*, and I'd scream again if he weren't choking me. He must realize I'm on the verge of passing out, because he lets go of my throat, returning his palm to my mouth. Every time he fucks into me, it's brutal. Painful. Carnal. He's hurting me, but I don't want him to stop. I want him to fuck me like this until it kills us both.

I'm so wet. He's so violent. Every time he thrusts, I'm on the brink of coming.

"Don't you dare come until I say so," he says, his eyes locked on mine. "I'm not done with you yet."

A small whine of protest escapes my throat before I can tamp it down. I'm so close it aches, even though the hard wall behind me makes my back hurt, the bite of pain distracting enough to stop me from fully letting go.

"Is this how Daddy's little whore wants to be fucked?" he asks. "In the dark, against the wall, like a fucking slut?"

My eyes widen when he says that. He takes his hand away from my mouth and continues to rut into me, his eyes burning into mine, demanding an answer. His words should offend me. But I suppose the truth hurts, right? My father *is* whoring me out, literally, to the highest bidder. A billionaire with a penchant for marrying equally rich teenage girls, whether they like him or not.

But instead of being offended by Will, I'm fucking turned on. "Yes," I moan.

"Yes, what? Say it."

Will's eyes are fire, his grip a vise.

"*Ohmygod*. Yes! This is how I want to be f-fucked," I gasp.

Will leans down and sucks my left nipple into his mouth, biting down hard enough to make me squeal. "Fuck!" I protest.

"Say it properly. Say, *this is how Daddy's little whore wants to be fucked*. And then I'll let you come."

I draw in a ragged breath, everything over-whelming me. Will pinches my other nipple in warning. "Say it."

Shame and lust flood every cell of my body as I repeat the words. "This is how Daddy's little whore wants to be fucked," I moan. Will sucks on my neck hard, hard enough to leave a bruise, and then he fucking *bites* me.

"Ahh!" I yell, watching him as he pulls his teeth away and kisses me on the mouth. He catches my bottom lip between his teeth and bites down, not enough to draw blood, but enough that it fucking hurts. At the same time, he presses his thumb to my clit and rubs rough circles. His anger thrills through me, the sudden violence welcome, and it's more than enough to lift me up past the pain.

I break apart before him, every part of me tightening, fireworks behind my heavy-lidded eyes.

He moves faster, fucks harder, until he's done. Suddenly I'm on my feet again, empty, my thighs damp, watching as the only boy I've ever really loved staggers back a step, hatred in his eyes and the remnants of our fuck shining on his cock.

"I can't marry you," I blurt out. "It's too late." *I need to get out of here.* "I'm s-sorry. I have to go."

Will laughs, but the sound is devoid of any joy. "Do I *look* like I'm finished yet?"

I turn and take a step back, bracing my hand on the smooth wall we were just up against. I know if I really want to leave, he won't stop me. But maybe I'm not ready for this to be over, either.

"Fuck," he hisses, his eyes fixed on my thigh. I follow his gaze, to the sticky semen rolling down my inner thigh. "Do you have any idea what that does to me? Seeing my cum on you like that? Knowing some other asshole gets to do that to you?"

I'm going to be late to my own birthday party. My

father will be pacing his office right about now, wondering where I am. At the hotel, flowers will be hung, crystal glasses polished, the rooftop pool beside the ballroom heated to the perfect temperature, even though nobody will be swimming tonight. Everything will be on schedule. Except me. Because I'm too busy standing in a mausoleum full of my dead family, naked, with cum leaking out of me.

It's kind of fucking awful when I think about it like that. But it's my party, and I'll be late if I want to. Will's erection shows no signs of going away, and I'll probably never see him again after we get in our respective cars and leave this place today.

And I love him.

So, fuck it.

Daddy can wait.

Wordlessly, I reach down and run my finger through the creamy liquid on my thigh, all the while acutely aware of Will's concentrated gaze. I bring the same finger to my mouth and suck, my pussy throbbing in anticipation as Will sucks in a sharp breath.

"Turn around and put your hands on the fucking altar," he demands, his eyes almost black in the weak light. Black and predatory. Lust alights in my belly anew, but I don't obey.

Rage keeps his dick hard as he spins me around,

his big palm on the side of my face as he pushes my cheek into the cold marble of the altar. A few meters away, on the other end of the hard table, our two candles burn, streaks of wax tumbling down the fat pillars. I watch them, mesmerized, as Will's cock splits me again. It's even deeper like this, him fucking me from behind, and I moan as he fucks me so hard I almost pass out.

It hurts, this way, him so deep, so punishing, that he bottoms out against my cervix every time he drives his hips into me. I squeeze my eyes shut, pain and pleasure a singular feeling now, no clear line where one ends and the other begins. Will lays his big body over me, his chest slick with sweat against my back as he licks along the shell of my ear.

"He can put you in that ivory tower, but you'll have to leave eventually," he whispers in my ear. "And when you do, I'm fucking taking you. I'll take you away and lock you up so nobody can have you except *me*." He pulls out of me, pressing the tip of his cock to my ass. I stiffen. I've never done that before.

"This does not belong to Augustus Capulet, do you understand? Not him, not Joshua Grayson, not any of those fucks. This is *mine*," he says, pushing insistently against the tight ring of muscle. He reaches both hands around and pinches my nipples, hard.

"These are mine." And finally, he slides back inside my pussy. "This is mine," he repeats, reaching around to pinch my clit. It's enough to make me come again, and as I tighten around him, a long moan dragging from my lungs, he comes, too, fucking me so hard I'm not sure I'll be able to walk on my high heels tonight.

We lie there for several moments, both catching our breath, Will's breath hot on my exposed skin. Finally, he pulls away from me, and I press my legs together to stop any more sticky liquid leaking down my leg. The last thing I need is to worry about leaving a puddle of jizz on the mausoleum floor. I'm already going to hell for what we just did in here.

"Here," Will says gruffly, throwing my dress on the altar beside me. I straighten, with some difficulty, my body used and abused and feeling boneless, floaty.

"Thank you," I say quietly, drawing the dress over my head. Will zips up the back of the dress, his movements slow, almost reluctant. I fiddle with my hair, locate my shoes and hold them on hooked fingers, and then, finally, I've run out of reasons not to face him.

I turn and face the man whose heart I've just ripped out, shame and guilt rising with the blood in my cheeks. Will's waiting patiently, just as he always has, his gaze hooded, suspicious. He looks fine, not a crease on his shirt, not a hair out of place, and I'm pretty sure I look like I've just been gang raped in a ghetto and left for dead.

"Tell me what happened today," he demands, zipping his pants up. "Everything."

I swallow. I need some water. And a case of wine. A faked death and a new identity wouldn't hurt.

Goddamn it.

"Joshua was in my father's office this morning," I say tiredly. "He left a ring."

"A ring," Will repeats.

"An engagement ring," I clarify. "For tonight."

Will's entire body seems to shake. He's so fucking angry, it's a wonder he doesn't start smashing his fists into the walls. "Avery," he says, his tone terrifying. He's never hurt me before, but he's never looked like this before, either. I can see the way his fists are balled up, the brutal fucking *rage*, and if a Cartier box could make a bruise on my face, imagine what a man's anger could do.

"This isn't over," he seethes. "We're not done here."

I don't answer, but I guess the look on my face is answer enough.

He stares at me for a long moment, shaking his head. He opens his mouth to say something else, but he must change his mind, because the next minute, I'm alone.

He's gone. I blink through tears, sliding to the floor, curling my legs around beside me as I stare up at the plaques that mark the final resting places of my sister, my mother, and my stillborn brother, the longed-for son whose entry into this world ended both of their lives.

All three of them dead because they were born Capulets.

Not just a surname, not just a bloodline — but a curse.

I stare up at my sister's spot in the wall, at eye-level if I were standing. Adeline would know what to do. She always knew what to do. That's why her suicide was even more tragic. Death was the only logical choice for her.

I don't want to die. I'm too weak to pull the trigger and end it all, too much of a coward to put my head underwater and let cold death rush into my lungs.

I understand Will's warring love and hatred, I do. It's exactly the feeling that claws at my throat whenever I think of my sister and what she doomed me to in her absence. It's exactly the sensation that fills me when my father kisses my cheek, and I melt into his carefully doled out ration of affection like an emotionally malnourished child, even as I want to kill him with my bare hands for using me like a worthless pawn in our family's name.

CHAPTER THREE

ROME

*H*ave you ever tried getting your dick sucked after you've been snorting yourself stupid for three days?

It's all milk and cookies on day one, all warm and soft and lovely. But after a while ... After a while, it just *hurts*.

"Rosaline," I mumble. My hands are on her head, but there's so much loose blonde hair that I can't find her face.

It's day three of a sex-and-drugs bender that should have ended before it began, when Rosaline called me on Friday night. I'm still not sure why I answered, but you can probably blame my aforementioned dick for that.

This girl is insatiable. She's so pale, her small,

firm tits firm in my palms as she bounces in my lap. We've moved to fucking now that her jaw is sore. Rosaline's pussy is tight enough. My dick is hard enough. It's all vaguely pleasant. And yet ... it's like sandpaper against my skin at the same time. I'm too high to come. I'm like an engine revving at eighty percent, but my handbrake is jammed on, and I'm not getting anywhere. And goddamn it, her *hair*. It's everywhere. There are strands on my couch and on my clothes and earlier, when I swallowed a mouthful of the beer she'd handed me, one of those strands got stuck halfway down my fucking throat and made me gag. She's got so many hair extensions weaved into her head, if she committed a crime a lot of innocent Russian women would be going to prison.

"Rosaline," I snap, pushing her off my lap.

"What are you doing?" she asks, toppling to the side of me, landing on a pile of cushions at the far end of my long, antique leather couch.

I put myself back together, wincing as I tuck my thoroughly-fucked cock back into my jeans and button up. I fasten my belt, too, selecting a notch one tighter than normal. What is it about girls who get high and suddenly turn into sex-crazed demons?

Though, to be fair, Rosaline is a sex-crazed

demon when she's straight. Can't blame the coke for her insatiable libido.

Rosaline leans back on my leather couch, the only nice thing in this falling-down room. Her eyes are red-rimmed and empty. She's fucking high, and her comedown is yet to kick in. *Oh honey, just you wait. The higher you go, the further you fall.*

"I'm tired," I say, my only explanation. I stretch my arms above my head and let them fall out to the sides, my head resting on the low back of the couch. I'm an offering on an imaginary cross, a crucifixion of my very own making. Because I'm starting to come down off this shit … and the fall is brutal.

Rosaline pouts beside me. She's still flying high, her eyes like a cat stalking in the middle of the night. She straddles me again, placing her hands on the back of the couch, lifting herself into a position where she can graze her nipples against my lips. She rubs herself all over me like a sex-starved devil, as if we haven't just been screwing for days, and when I don't take the bait, she pushes off me dramatically.

"You hunt me down in a bar, bring me to your piece of shit house, I let you fuck me *in the ass*, and this is the thanks I get?"

I laugh. "This house is not a piece of shit," I reply. I would be offended, but it kind of is a piece of shit.

"And I seem to remember you begging earlier for me to — well, you know."

Her eyes narrow. "Think you're so fucking cool, living in a house that's falling down around you, just to spite people who've forgotten you exist." She jerks her thumb over her shoulder, toward the large bay window, and the estate that is basically a modern castle on the lot next door.

"Ouch," I say, holding my hand to my chest as if she's wounded me.

She rolls her eyes in response.

"Trust me," I say, staring at the rose garden that flanks the Capulet residence next door. The rose garden they keep finding snakes in during the summer, when the damn things slither through my uncut jungle of lawn and spook their horses in the stables out back. "They haven't forgotten."

"Well, I might be forgetting you," she snaps. "I need a fucking Uber." She stands up, twisting her knotted blonde hair in her fingers. "You fucking idiot, is this cum in my hair? These extensions cost me three thousand dollars!"

Her comedown has arrived. Rosaline gets nasty when she's strung out. Also, if she's really paying that much for her hair, she's being ripped off something wicked.

"Oops," I deadpan, spreading my palms. "In my defense, your hair is impossible to escape, Rosie. It's literally everywhere." I pick a strand off my pants and hold it up to prove my point.

"Don't call me Rosie, you fucking perv. Rosie is a child's name."

"Well, you're kind of acting like a child," I reply. "Does that count?"

She huffs.

I raise my eyebrows, letting out a laugh. My throat is dry from all the drugs, and I end up sounding like an old man, coughing and wheezing at the end.

"Holy shit, I need some water."

"They have running water in real houses," Rosaline says, taking a little plastic container out of her purse and placing it on the mirrored coffee table. I side-eye her as she pulls out a tiny baggie of brown powder, a spoon, and a neatly wrapped syringe.

"What the fuck are you doing?" I ask her, snatching the baggie from her hand. Her eyes go wide; she thinks I'm stealing her shit.

"You can have it back when you leave," I promise. "You like cheesy crust on your pizza?"

"Don't take my shit and offer me pizza," she seethes. "Give me that." Her skinny arm shoots out, her hand trying to rip the baggie of brown powder from my hand, but I'm stronger.

"No heroin in my house. Ever," I say, shoving the bag in my jeans pocket. "You can have this back when you leave. Unless you're leaving now?" *Please leave now, you crazy bitch.*

She hesitates. "I want to stay with you. But I'm not eating pizza. Carbs make me bloat."

I look at her tiny frame dubiously. "We haven't eaten in three days," I say to her.

She smiles deviously. "You can eat me again," she says, pointing at her red lace panties.

"Rosaline," I say slowly, enunciating every syllable. "No more sex. No more drugs! I'm. Ordering. *Pizza*. What do you want?"

"One more bump," she says, smiling sweetly at me. She's a pretty girl, but I wish she wouldn't smile. Her teeth are pointed like a cat's, and when she grins, she looks like a damn bloodthirsty vampire, angling for my jugular. "And order me a green salad."

I shake my head, pulling my cellphone out and dialing. I order the pizza, complete with cheesy crust, and a fucking green salad on the side. My stomach growls angrily as I end the call, just in time to see a river of red liquid erupt from Rosaline's face.

"What the fuck!?" I yell. She's got a blank expression on her face, blood pouring from her nostrils, and ladies and gentlemen, this is what happens when you have one more bump after three days of snorting and fucking. Your nostrils decide to give up the fight, and bleed like fucking fire hydrants full of red paint.

"My sofa," I say. She's oblivious. "Rosaline. Get off my fucking sofa!" I stare down at her in dismay, watching as she stains the only decent thing that I own outside of this property, this rambling decrepit mess that the fuckers next door keep trying to have declared uninhabitable. Not my sofa. Anything but my sofa.

"I need the bathroom," Rosaline says. Still not moving. Desperate, I go around behind her and hook my arms under her shoulders, basically dragging her to the bathroom. We leave a red trail down the hallway, making me wince. It looks like somebody just got murdered here.

I carry her into the downstairs bathroom and help her into the tub, turning the taps on full. Rosaline screams when freezing cold water hits her thighs, trying to scramble out of the bath. I keep one hand firmly planted on her shoulder, to stop her from thrashing around like a wet cat, as I locate the plug and shove it into the hole in the bottom of the tub.

"Running water," I say, shaking my head in mock surprise. "Who'd have thought?"

"No hot water," she whimpers, her lips a little blue around the edges.

"Mmm, it's practically barbaric," I muse. "You poor thing. Don't you dare die, you hear me?"

She smiles, trying to cup my chin with her blood-stained hand. "Aww, you're so sweet."

I pull my face out of her reach. "Your blood is literally all over my house. If you die, it'll be like CSI: Verona Heights in here. And guess who they'll be arresting?"

The water is covering her legs now, and Rosaline seems to be adjusting to the temperature. I've even added a little hot water to take off the edge. I'm not completely heartless.

"Stay in there until the bleeding stops," I instruct her, heading for the door. I let out a groan when I see the crime scene left in her wake, sinking down onto the un-bloodied end of my couch as I survey the destruction around me. Empty wine and whiskey bottles in the corner. My mirrored coffee table, still laden with fat caterpillars of speed, waiting to be snorted up. Bright red drops of blood amongst the white powder, blood and smack, looking disturbingly similar to pizza flour and pasta sauce. Gross. This mess was *so* not worth it.

I sit there for a few minutes, lighting a cigarette. I watch through the large bay windows as a limousine snakes up the long driveway next door. I wonder if it's *her*. Probably. It's her birthday today, and there'll be a party or some other fancy shit going on. The thought of a bunch of rich assholes standing on the balconies and in the rose garden next door and eyeing off my fire-damaged piece of shit makes anger burn in my belly. I should crash the party. I should drown Rosaline in their fucking pool while everyone watches. I'd drown her in mine, but the pool in my backyard is a swamp now, reserved only for mosquitoes to breed and hatch their babies. I'm daydreaming about sneaking into the party next door later tonight when Rosaline suddenly appears beside me, like a silent ninja, her face still streaked with blood. I put my hand on the Glock that sits on the side table beside me, my fingers wrapped around the butt of the gun before I realize it's her, and not an intruder.

"Jesus fucking Christ," I say, my heart rate spiking like I've just been hit with a dose of adrenalin — or snorted a line, I guess.

"I have to get out of here," Rosaline mumbles, snatching up her handbag and making a beeline for the bathroom again. I frown, puzzled by her sudden change of heart. My suspicion grows as she closes the bathroom door again, and I hear muted rummaging.

Fucking bitch. I know exactly what she's doing.

I drag my phone out of my jeans pocket, shoot off a text.

Bitch is in my bathroom trying to steal my stash.

Three little bubbles pop up under my message right away.

I'm in your driveway. Want me to bring the crew?

Can I eat this pizza, then?

One ear still on Rosaline in the bathroom, I reply.

No. Let's keep this between us. Bring the pizza. I'm starved.

Rosaline exits the bathroom, stepping around her own trail of nose-blood with bare feet. She looks like a dead corpse walking.

"Rosie," I say sweetly, kicking back on my couch. "I thought you wanted to stay?"

She smiles. "I need to get home, freshen up. Call you later?"

I don't even need to look in my bathroom to know that she found my stash and stole it. You know why? Because Rosaline would never, ever leave her heroin in my jeans pocket, forgotten, let alone a small mountain of white powder on my coffee table. She's the kind of girl who would scoop it up and store it in her cheeks to get it past the front door.

Speaking of.

There's a knock at the front door.

"Pizza delivery!" the voice at the door calls.

"Can you let the pizza guy in on the way out?"

Rosaline grins, her pupils the size of dinner plates. "Sure thing, babe," she coos, tucking her suspiciously full handbag under her arm and making a beeline for the front door.

She opens the door, her free hand out to grab the pizza, when she freezes. "Merc?" she says, her hand stopped in mid-air. I'm on my feet at the same time, moving across the large, open space to the open door.

"Pizza!" my best friend says jovially, throwing two boxes of cheesy crust pizza on the floor beside Rosaline. "You want to pay with cash, or with the shit you just stole?"

Rosaline tries to scurry around Merc, with no success. Merc crosses his arms over his broad chest, smiling, revealing two rows of perfect white teeth that look even brighter against his Hispanic coloring. Rosaline turns suddenly, probably headed for an alternative exit, but instead barreling right into my open arms. I get her in a bear hug, pinning her arms at her sides as Merc snatches her purse from her hand. He pulls out a metal cigarette box, a skull stamped on the front, and snaps it open to reveal rows of bright red heart-shaped pills.

My pills.

Rosaline starts to panic. "I can explain," she says, trying to pull away from me. I respond by tightening my hold on her, picking her up off her feet and heading back to the bathroom.

---

*T*en minutes later, I'm chewing on cheesy crust pepperoni pizza, and Rosaline is tied to one of my kitchen chairs, sitting in the middle of my living room, furious as she tries to yell at me past the piece of tape over her mouth.

It's not the first time I've tied a half-naked girl to a chair and threatened her life, and I very much doubt it'll be the last. Chicks, man. Sometimes the only way to get them to tell the truth is to show them the sharp end of a knife, make them cry a little. Merc finishes his slice before me, dusting his hands on his jeans as he retrieves a switchblade from his pocket and opens it with a metallic *snick* sound.

"Hey Rosie, you ready to talk?" Merc asks.

I hold up a slice of pizza. "You tell me who you're stealing for, I'll even share my pizza with you."

If this were an episode of Supernatural, her eyes would be solid black right now, little demon she is. Fortunately, this is reality, and Rosaline isn't a demon — just a very fucking shady girl, one I should have known would bring me a whole bunch of trouble that I don't need.

Merc unceremoniously rips the tape from her mouth, and probably takes half of the skin on her face along with it. Her eyes pop a little from the pain, as she gasps in a breath. "Motherfucker," she spits, pulling at her bindings. "I'm going to make sure you both get what's coming to you for this."

I raise my eyebrows. "Rosaline, you tried to steal my entire stash of pills. Pills that are very special to me. The least you can do is tell me who you're stealing it for."

Her eyes constantly shift between Merc and I, probably trying to figure out which one of us she can sweet talk the fastest. She hones in on Merc, licking her lips as she parts her thighs, her very short skirt riding up as she flashes her panty-less crotch before she crosses her legs. Merc sits on the sofa beside me, leaning forward, a frown etched into his forehead as he points to Rosaline with the switchblade.

"Did you just try to Basic Instinct me, Rosaline?" Merc asks. "Seriously? Put it away. Tell me who sent you to steal Rome's pills."

Rosaline starts hurling abuse at both of us, unintelligible nonsense peppered with curse words and high-pitched screaming. Merc rolls his eyes, slapping the tape back on her mouth.

We both stand over her.

"What do we do now?" Merc asks.

I shrug. "Torture her until she tells us who she's working for."

CHAPTER FOUR

AVERY

*a*n hour to go.

I am a master of denial, but we're getting right down to the wire now. I'm standing on a little raised podium in the presidential suite of the Palatial Hotel, just another of my family's business holdings that are scattered across California, but I like this place. It's rooted in my memory almost as much as my family home, maybe even more. This is the place my mother loved to bring us to get us out of the house. She always loved being in the bustle of a busy city, not cooped up at home, where good wives are supposed to stay. My parents were married in a Catholic church, but they had their reception here. Every significant event that wasn't held at home has happened in this place, and now it's my turn, so why do I feel like I'm about to die?

Maybe because I am.

Not literally, of course. I very much doubt anybody's going to kill me. I am the golden goose of the family, after all. Have to take care of me so I keep laying those golden eggs. Ironic, isn't it, after what I learned this afternoon?

My dress is stunning, and that almost makes it worse. It's so beautiful, but my mother will never see it, or my sister. The people who will see it are strangers, and men who think they can control every little facet of my life. I can't stop thinking about Will, about the way he left. He's the kind of boy who likes to make a scene, and I wonder if that's what he has planned for tonight.

I hear my father's footsteps in the hallway before I see him, but I know it's him. When you're rich like us, there is a certain way that you hold yourself, a way that you walk. I would know my father's footsteps anywhere. Maybe it's because we're the only two who've been roaming around our empty mansion for the last nine years, ever since Adeline died. Nathan and his parents were around a lot of the time, but they'd always go home eventually, and it was just me and Daddy again, quiet like mice, the house echoing with our movements like it knew it was too big for just two people.

Daddy's footsteps are unmistakable, and they get heavier, closer. I look at myself in the long mirror, adjusting little bits of fabric here and there. The whole thing is attached to me by a series of pins.

Even though the party starts in an hour, it has to fit exactly. There can be no loose threads, no empty spaces. This gown will sit against my skin because I'm being sewn into it right now. There's no zipper. At the end of the night, I'll unpick the seams, unwind myself from this mess of tulle and lace, and then I'll probably burn the dress.

"You look beautiful, darling," my father says through gritted teeth. "Beautiful, and late. I was about to start driving the streets looking for you. Where the *hell* have you been?"

I don't respond. I'm still too angry with him to even look him in the eye.

"Avery," he presses.

I grimace, seeing myself in the mirror as I make the expression. I don't look very nice when I do that.

"Don't give yourself a coronary, Augie," I simper. "I was with Will. Remember Will?"

My father narrows his eyes. "That's the thing

about guys like Will, honey. Nobody remembers them once they're gone."

I huff out a breath. "You're unbelievable."

Daddy rolls his eyes. "So I've been told." He tilts his head, taking in my dress, my hair, like I'm some sort of product he's about to unveil. "Did you tell Will about the engagement?"

I blink, forcing myself to remain impassive. No tears. He doesn't deserve them. "Yes. I told him."

My father seems pleased by this. "And?"

I smile, the gesture poisonous, as I reach out to straighten my father's tie. "And he got very angry. He said I was my daddy's little whore. And then he fucked me. With no protection."

I pause for a beat.

"*Twice.*"

My father turns the brightest shade of pink imaginable, smacking my hand away from his tie as I fix my expression to resting bitch face, the smirk on my bright red lips the only thing to give away my mood.

"Careful, Avery. Don't push me."

I roll my eyes. "Or what? You'll marry me off to a man of your choosing? Withhold my trust fund fund until the marriage is consummated? Or maybe you'll steal my fucking eggs and make test tube babies with them without my knowledge."

Daddy scowls.

"Oh, that's right! You already did all that. You already destroyed any chance I had at ever having a real life. So give me one good reason why I shouldn't just do what Adeline did, huh? Tell me. One reason."

Daddy's jaw twitches.

"Do you even love me, Daddy?" I ask, in a pathetically small voice. "You've barely said it to me, even when I was a little girl. *Do you*?"

Daddy opens his mouth to reply, his expression stricken. But no words come out. *He'll be so angry. I shouldn't have said that.*

But then my father does something I've never seen him do before. Augustus Capulet, a man I've seen kill with his bare hands, when he thought I wasn't watching. Augustus Capulet, the man who showed not an ounce of emotion at any of the funerals of his wife and children. Augustus Capulet, the most powerful — and most feared — man in California, blinks heavily, a single tear sliding down his cheek.

"More than the world," he says, his voice breaking. "More than *anything*."

Something inside me withers and dies. My father loves me, and he's still sentencing me to this cruel travesty? It would have been better if he'd just said no.

"How can you do this to me if you love me?" I whisper.

My father steps forward suddenly, his broad arms wrapping around me, pinning my arms to my sides. He rests his head on my shoulder, since I'm taller than him standing on this little podium, and he holds me to him so hard it hurts me. After a moment, I let my head fall heavy to the side, resting atop his head.

"It's not too late to stop this," I whisper. "*Dad.*"

Daddy pulls away from me, wiping his face hastily. He smiles sadly, cupping my face in both of his palms, his eyes burning into mine as I search his gaze for some kind of hope. It's madness to believe he'll put a stop to what's about to happen, but I'm hardly sane anyway.

"When you were a baby," he says, his chin trembling, "I never knew what to do with you. Neither did your mother. We were spoilt rich kids who'd never held a baby before your sister was born. And she was so calm. She never cried. She slept when she was supposed to sleep, ate when she was supposed to eat, and smiled any time we pointed a camera at her. And then you came along, and we just assumed you would be like her."

I'm bewildered. My father never speaks about memories, or our childhoods, anything.

"You came into this world screaming bloody murder," Daddy continues, smiling proudly. "From the minute you drew breath, Avery, you've been a fighter. I knew you would be the one to take over the world, and so did you. You took over our world, and you made it very clear that you would always fight for what you wanted. Your mother and I didn't know what to do with you. The only person who made you happy was your sister. That giant house with all its rooms and you weren't happy unless she was in your crib, sleeping beside you. And she *adored* you. She would always say that you weren't our baby, that you were hers. She was the only one who knew what you needed when you cried, while your mother and I stood by like we were part of the furniture."

Hearing about Adeline and our mom makes me cry. I look up at the ceiling, trying to preserve my makeup before tears spill over and onto my cheeks.

"You are all I have," Daddy says emphatically, catching a tear with his thumb before it can touch my cheek. "You mean more to me than anything, even if I'm incapable of showing it. Please trust me. There are things far worse than marrying Joshua, and I can't protect you if you don't do this."

"Things far worse? Come on," I scoff.

My father's face loses any trace of the emotion he

displayed just a second ago. "Would you prefer to be married to somebody worse? Would you?"

"Who could be worse than a forty-year-old man who was a teenager before I was even born?" I demand. "He's old enough to be my father. Doesn't that disgust you?"

Daddy tenses. "Not as much as the thought of you marrying Tyler Capulet. Do you really want to marry your psychotic cousin? Because if you don't marry Joshua, my darling, who do you think the family has lined up in his place?"

I'm stunned. Tyler is a full-blown psychopath. He's an efficient hitman, a fabulous family representative to keep the drug cartels in line — because he's insane. Literally and unequivocally.

"Think about it," my father mutters. "A headstrong wife like you would be dead inside a year if you were married to that little prick. But Avery, if you want to take your chances on your rapey cokehead of a cousin — by all means, now is the time to speak up."

Daddy looks at his watch. "I can call my sister now, tell her to bring Tyler's suit and tie. And her son, of course. Just say the word."

I swallow thickly, fresh panic rising in my throat.

Daddy doesn't know what Ty did to me when we were younger. Or does he?

"You know what he did to me, don't you?" I whisper. "The night Addy died?"

My father's face reddens, as he nods.

"Who told you?"

Daddy lets out a deep breath. "Who do you think?"

"Nathan?"

Daddy raises his eyebrows. "Trying to get Nathan to tell me anything is like trying to get blood out of the cream-leather seats in a Mercedes Benz."

Realization stabs into me. "Rome."

"Rome Montague," Daddy concedes.

I shake my head. "He promised he wouldn't tell anyone."

"I'm pretty sure he changed his mind when he saw Tyler sitting beside you at Adeline's funeral," Daddy says. "It was the right thing for him to do. Tyler Capulet hasn't been welcomed into our home or our businesses since I almost killed him at your sisters wake." He tucks a strand of hair behind my ear. "Just because you don't know what I do to keep you safe, doesn't mean I'm doing nothing. Some things are better left unsaid."

I step down from the little podium, going to stand

by the window. From here, I can see the afternoon sun, dipping low on the horizon. In an hour, it'll be swallowed up by night. In less than that time, I'll be swallowed up by my destiny.

"Will was so sad, Daddy," I murmur, putting my fingers against the window, looking over the city that will soon be mine, even though I don't want it. "You should have seen him. He was … it was like something broke inside him. I broke it. And I didn't want to."

I can feel my father approach behind me. "Sometimes we hurt the ones we love," he offers, and I know he's referring to himself and his actions as much as mine.

"Did you hurt Mom?" I whisper. "Did she hurt you?"

Daddy puts his hands on my shoulders, turning me gently to face him. I don't resist. I'd much rather stay in this room forever, even if it means talking about difficult things, than go out there and face the music.

"Your mother and I were very lucky, Avery. We knew each other from childhood. Our parents had decided early on that we would be a good match. We grew up together. We went to the same schools, we moved in the same circles. Your mother was my best friend before she was anything else. We didn't even go on a date until we were both eighteen, but we were still brought up with the understanding that we would be married one day."

"How lovely for you to not have to go through this bullshit," I say, but there's no conviction behind my words.

"We tried with you and Rome," Daddy says, a darkness passing over his features momentarily as he looks away. "We didn't realize things with the Montagues would go … the way they did."

"Yeah, hindsight's a real bitch, isn't it?" I say. Daddy spreads his palms and shrugs as if to say, *what do you want me to do*?

"Dad."

"Avery."

"I want to marry Will."

"No," Daddy snaps.

"Dad!" I raise my voice, tossing my hair over my shoulder, forgetting what it's hiding.

Daddy sees the bruise on my neck, *thanks Will*, and shakes his head, reaching his fingers out to touch it. "He *did* hurt you."

I rip his hand away from my neck. "All he did was give me a damn hickey, Father. It didn't hurt at all. *You* hurt me. *You* used me. You continue to use me. It's not *fair*."

"Life's not fair," he grinds out.

"I don't want to talk about it anymore," I say, turning away, headed for the door. I need to find Jennifer before this thing starts.

"Do you trust me?" Daddy asks, still at the window behind me.

My shoulders droop. "Yes. No. *I don't know*," I whisper.

Joshua Grayson takes the opportunity to knock on the open door, entering with the worst timing ever for the second time in one day.

"Augustus. Avery." He nods to each of us in greeting, a smile stretching over his tanned face, a little dimple in one cheek that I've never noticed before. I wonder if our children will inherit that dimple. I wonder how quickly I could find a sharp object to stab into Joshua's cheek, right into that fucking dimple, so I never have to look at his smug smile again. I tilt my head to the side, taking him in. He looks incredible, actually, in a dark navy suit, tailored impeccably, a pair of cufflinks with the Capulet family crest stamped into them at his wrists. That irritates the hell out of me. It's like a buy-in of a stock portfolio. An acquisition. Buy the farm, drink all the milk you want for free. And I'm the cow, being fed up for the slaughter.

"Isn't it bad luck to see the bride before she walks down the aisle?" I snap, ignoring his attempt at cordial conversation. Really, I just want him to go away.

"I think that's the wedding," Joshua replies, nonplussed by my snark, looking like he stepped out of a men's aftershave commercial.

I shrug. It's all the same to me.

"I just came in to see how you're holding up, Avery," Joshua says. Jesus, he'd be the best salesman. If I didn't loathe him so much, I'd melt into a puddle under his stare. Some people are just born with this charisma that pours off them wherever they go. My father had it, before Mom died, and he can still turn it on when business demands it. Adeline had it, too. She could sell you anything just by batting her eyelids. Me? Not so much. The terms standoffish and Ice Queen have been thrown my way more than once in my life.

"As well as can be expected," I reply.

"Your dress is stunning," he adds. "Fit for a queen."

I smile icily. "Thank you. It belonged to my sister." A lie, but whatever. I'm not going to let

Joshua forget this business arrangement of his used to have a different Capulet sister attached.

"Avery," Daddy says sharply.

Joshua lets the dead-sister-you-almost-married comment roll off him. I almost feel sorry for him. He's waited a long time and invested a lot of energy and cash just to be married to a fucking bitch like me.

"I'm sure she'd say the same if she were here," he says smoothly.

Daddy clears his throat. "Looks like Jennifer did a fabulous job, getting everything ready for the event."

"Oh, we're doing small talk now, are we?" I reply. "Are we going to pretend that Joshua didn't hear that whole conversation in your office this morning? Because I didn't get that memo. I should check my emails before we go out there."

"Avery, for God's sake," my father says. "Come on, now. I had no way of knowing what my brother was going to say to you earlier. Don't punish Joshua for Enzo's big mouth."

"Oh my God. It's not even about that," I fire back. "You betrayed me. You lied to me, and you didn't even tell me. What kind of father does that to a sixteen-year-old girl? What kind of man goes along with such a thing?"

Joshua's eyebrows rise slightly, and he puts his

palms up in a supplicating gesture. "I'm going to leave you two to finish getting ready. Avery, you look lovely. I've scheduled all day tomorrow so we can meet up and talk about everything that's on your mind. I'm not the villain, okay?"

I stare at him blankly, until my father steps toward me and wraps one arm around my shoulders in a suffocating hug that screams: *behave.*

"I'm busy tomorrow," I reply. "What a shame."

"Oh, that doctor's appointment? Something about an IUD? I had my secretary talk to your assistant. It's been rescheduled for next week."

And then the smug motherfucker gives us both the most dazzling grin, complete with a wave, and closes the door behind him.

It's happening again. My dress, which was a little loose before, is suddenly all too tight. It constricts me, pressing up against my ribs, squeezing the air out of my lungs.

"What the FUCK?" I seethe. I turn on my father. "I hate him," I spit, gesturing wildly at the closed door. "I HATE him!"

I don't even see the open palm coming at me. My face feels the sting as my father slaps me across the face hard enough that I make a choking sound in my throat. "*Ow.*"

"I'm sorry," Daddy says, straightening my hair as I hold my smarting cheek. "I didn't know what else to do to snap you out of this state you're in."

I blink, once, twice, and then without thinking, I hit him back. Right across his freshly-shaved cheek. It probably hurts me more than him, my palm buzzing angrily as I watch a red mark rise on his cheek.

"Feel better?" he murmurs.

I shrug, feeling embarrassed. "A little."

"Your self-defense is getting sloppy," Daddy remarks. "You never used to hit like a girl."

"I'm usually hitting inanimate objects, not my father," I mutter.

"If you say so."

"You need to leave," I say to my father. "You need to get out of my face now, because if you don't, I am going to lose my fucking mind."

My father sets his teeth inside his jaw so hard, I can see the vein in his forehead throb.

"Fine," Daddy says. "I'll see you out there, I suppose."

"I suppose you will," I reply sharply.

"And Avery," Daddy adds, always needing the last word. "Don't get any ideas. Don't try to run off. Just do as you're told, for once in your life."

And he slams the door.

I look back to the mirror, breathing deeply, letting the calm wash back over me. I've already cried enough today to last me the rest of my life. After I left the cemetery, with black eyeliner all over my face, I went straight home, sat on the floor of my shower, and cried. It was probably a good thing that it happened the way it did. I can't imagine Will's face if the engagement had been announced at the party. In fact, I'm pretty sure he would have killed Joshua Grayson with his bare hands if he could. Thank goodness for small miracles, I guess.

Then again, maybe it would have been a good thing if Will had spared me from having to marry such a horrible man. I'm deep in an elaborate daydream about Will and Joshua, fighting to the death for me, when Nathan enters the room without knocking. He whistles as he takes me in. "You look good," he says.

"I should hope so," I reply. "After all, I'm the entertainment for the night."

"Poor little rich girl," Nathan says, stroking my hair, but I know he actually feels sorry for me.

I look at him pointedly. "What aren't you telling me?"

He shrugs. "It's nothing."

"Come on, spill," I say. "If I can't have any excitement in my life, at least I can live vicariously through you."

"Well, I might've met a girl."

"Really," I say. "And what might this girl's name be?"

"Never you mind about that," he replies. He pulls two travel brochures out of his back pocket. "Fiji or the Caribbean?" he says. I make a face. "Poor little rich boy," I mimic him. "Can't decide where to take your new bang buddy?"

He rolls his eyes. "Fiji it is."

It's then that I notice the small suitcase in the corner. "When are you leaving?" I ask, suddenly alarmed.

He shrugs. "Tomorrow, I guess. Whenever we can fire up the jet."

"Nathan, a Capulet jet is not going to take you all the way to Fiji. You have to get on a commercial flight for that."

"Ugh," he says, frowning. "I know, right? We're flying down to LAX in the company jet, meeting the commercial flight there. Peasants, they'll call us."

"Again," I say, "Poor little rich boy."

"I'll send you a postcard," he says.

"How about I just stow away in your luggage?" I suggest. "I think that would be less painful to everybody. Daddy can forge my signature on the marriage certificate, put one of my embryos in a gestational carrier. Jesus, I don't even need to be here at all."

Nathan starts fussing with my hair. "That's true," he says, "But you're forgetting the most important part."

"What's that?" I ask.

"The part where Joshua Grayson gets to wear you as arm candy."

"Isn't that what Photoshop is for?"

Nathan laughs. "I guess. Anyway, they're not going to let you leave the country, because we all know you'd never come back."

"Well, the least you can do is pick me up a souvenir, okay?"

"Done," Nathan says, moving my hair into the exact same style it was in when he started fussing with it.

"It's going to be fine, Avery," Nathan says, suddenly serious. "Just get through tonight, and take it as it comes. I don't even think it will be as bad as you think it is."

I turn on my little podium to face my cousin directly. "Nathan," I reply, "Come on, man. Don't bullshit me. You and I both know it's going to be worse."

CHAPTER FIVE

AVERY

*N*o more minutes left on the clock; we're at zero hour, here. No cataclysmic natural disaster has slit the earth and swallowed me whole; no superhero has swept in to rescue me.

This is *happening*.

I need somewhere to wipe my palms; but the puffy skirt of my gown doesn't seem appropriate.

"Avery Capulet, everyone!"

Five hundred pairs of eyes look my way as I sashay down the middle of the glass-ceilinged ballroom my father has decked out with nauseating arrays of flowers, of twinkling fairy lights and enough champagne to fill the San Francisco Bay that shimmers beyond the heights of our palatial hotel.

Really, that is what it's called: The Palatial Hotel.

Because it's like a damn palace built on the edge of the financial district, full of Austrian crystal chandeliers and Calcutta marble floors.

It's unseasonably hot in San Francisco this year, especially since we're in the middle of a heat wave. People in Southern California would probably laugh at us as they roast through their regular hundred-plus summer days, but in the North we're a little more acclimated to clouds and wind.

I could blame my sweaty palms on the heatwave, but it's crisp and cold inside the hotel's grand glass enclosure. Cold like a refrigerator. Like a morgue.

You're daydreaming again, Avery.

I take a deep breath and focus on my father's booming voice, forgetting about the crowd of family and my father's friends. I feel like a head of cattle being marched down a market to fetch the highest bidder. Because although this is merely my twenty-fifth birthday and not an auction; almost everybody is here for one reason.

Money.

My money.

The money that, according to the rules of our family's trust, cannot be accessed by women heirs until they marry.

Which is complete fucking bullshit. We're living

in the age of equality, yet, according to the Capulet decree, all women born bearing the Capulet name would be penniless unless they marry a man of their father's choosing.

Arranged marriage, in 2018? In America?

I almost wish somebody in the crowd would shoot me, put me out of my misery. Almost.

"Think of all that money," I hear somebody whisper as I walk through the middle of a parted crowd. I look in the direction of the voice, finding a guilty face staring straight back at me. Jacob Goldstein. Preppy guy, Ivy League, all that crap that people spend their lives and their fortunes making sure they've got. I went to high school with Jacob, the most exclusive preparatory school on the West Coast of the United States. He's been trying to get into my pants since his voice broke and I grew out of my sports bra. *Sorry, buddy, you were never on the shortlist.*

Yes, I am the only surviving child of the most powerful man in California. Daddy has enough collective money and assets to rival anyone on the Forbes rich list, but he prefers to be discreet with his riches. If for no other reason than the fact that his wealth isn't entirely honest. The Capulet family is the Rosthchild family of the criminal underworld. Only, instead of owning and controlling banks, we own and control other things.

Diamonds. Guns. Drugs.

And yes, hotels. Lots and lots of hotels. After all, you have to launder the money somewhere, right?

My family has so much money, you could never spend it all. It's not in any one account, or controlled by any one person, but we have enough money to burn piles of the stuff as tall as this building, and not miss it at all.

Many of the men eyeing me off in the crowd find that staggering wealth extremely attractive.

Me, I learned a long time ago that money doesn't mean much. Beyond granting you food, and shelter, and warmth, money doesn't do much at all. It doesn't hold you at night when your father is still working, always working. It doesn't help you trust anybody who might be a romantic possibility.

Money doesn't bring your mother back from the dead after she dies giving birth to your stillborn brother when you're twelve years old. Money doesn't suck the water out of your dead sister's lungs after she drowns herself to avoid taking the throne that was her birthright, not mine. Now I'm the consolation prize to all this.

Money: I'm about to have more of it than any of these greedy fucks could imagine.

And I don't want it.

Not a nickel. Not a penny. Not a dirty dollar bill.

But for my father, I will take it. I will assume the throne of the Capulet family. It's my destiny, whether I want it or not.

As I get closer to the front of the grand ballroom, I see Joshua standing beside my father and my uncle, all three of them dressed in their best fucking suits. Christ, all I need is a bouquet of flowers to hold, and this could actually be our wedding. It's basically a rehearsal for that very eventuality. I fight to keep my eyes on a spot behind Joshua's head, wondering what it would look like if somebody shot him in the face and blasted his brains all over the back wall of the room.

That sure would solve a couple of my most pressing issues.

I make it to the front of the room. There are speeches. The Cartier box makes it's own entrance, to much applause. *Lamb, meet slaughter.* Joshua smiles at me as he slides the giant rock onto my finger. And just like that, we are engaged. I am betrothed. I look at the cold diamond's surface, imagining the sweet relief my sister must have felt as she plunged into icy waters, emptied her lungs of air, opened her mouth and let herself drown to avoid this very moment, all those years ago.

CHAPTER SIX

ROME

*M*erc takes great pleasure in getting to babysit Rosaline. I wonder if I'll return home to find her missing fingers, or teeth, or her large intestine. Merc does so relish the sight of blood, especially when it's spilled in the names of loyalty and vengeance.

Me, I could go the rest of my life and be quite happy to never see the brutal reality of a bullet hole, a stab wound, a lip split from angry fists. I prefer the simple life, dabbling in my makeshift lab in the basement of a house I own in Alameda County, across the bridge and far away, where the watchful eyes of Verona can't reach, or at least, choose not to look.

On the passenger seat beside me, I have an odd

assortment of things; a gold masquerade mask, a change of clothes, a Glock pistol, a switchblade. I'm driving a fucking Prius, because a Prius is the least showy, most able to blend in vehicle I could think of. I'm smart, these days. I mean, in my youth, before I understood the importance of flying under the radar, I used to drive a fucking hearse around town.

I'm not even kidding.

But drugs and conspicuous cars don't mix, so I'm blending in, going five over the speed limit as I cruise over the Bay Bridge, a ninja in my white electric-powered dream.

I pull up at a nondescript warehouse in Oakland a little while later, parking in a loading zone. The sky is starting to fade, the evening air a little cooler as the sun under over the horizon. I do a quick check of my surroundings, looking for cops, enemies, anything that might interfere with my mission. A gun tucked into the waistband of my jeans, a handful of pills that look more like Pez candies in my pocket, a fresh stick of peppermint gum, and I'm good to go.

Head down, I circle around to the back of the warehouse and enter the loading dock's open roller door. There are three beefy security dudes just inside the dock, hidden from the street but apparent as soon as my eyes adjust to the dark interior of the window-less space. They all nod at me, holding Uzi's pointed at the floor, and I nod back in greeting, sliding the gold mask over my eyes as I make my well-worn path into what can only be described as a parallel universe in the middle of the industrial district.

I open a small door in the back of the empty loading dock, my eyes adjusting rapidly to the dark interior beyond. It's still light outside, the sun holding on for at least another thirty minutes before it's grand departure, but in here, it's midnight twenty-four hours a day. I breathe in, a smirk tugging at the corner of my mouth as I enter what can only be described as one, big, fucked-up fairytale-themed party, complete with Sleeping Beauty being projected onto the bare white-brick wall at the far end of the space. Translucent black sheets of gauzy silk hang suspended from the ceiling in different configurations, wrapping around low, circular daybeds that, ironically, will most likely never see the light of day. On low tables, platters of red toffee-dipped apples sit gleaming, and black rose petals are scattered on every available surface. Fat, round candles burn eagerly, some on the floor, others on tables and low walls, the entire room pulsing like a fire marshal's living nightmare.

I know exactly where to go, heading for the stair-well at the side of the room, past the silk-draped couches and the people in various states of undress lounging upon them. I see flashes of pert breast and round, smooth ass cheek, of spread thighs and pistoning hips. Still, it's all fairly sedate down here on the ground floor, where people know they can be seen. It's up the stairs that I take, bouncing two at a time in my sneakers, that the real deviants are hiding out.

More security. A long, dark corridor that leads to a series of private rooms, criss-crossed along the walk-way. All locked. I stroll past two more security guards on my way down the hallway, looking at each door carefully. My reputation precedes me. There are little red stickers, the size of my thumbnail, stuck to every single door. Some rooms have three and four of the little dots. Each dot represents a customer wanting to purchase my wares, and this isn't exactly the type of thing you can just buy off the street corner. No, the drug I sell is exclusive. But it does have a rabid following, and as I enter the first door, this one adorned with three red stickers, I have to fight to keep the amused grin off my face.

The rooms in this place are identical, lavish but

minimalist, outfitted with everything you could ever want for your own personal sex-and-booze bender. Chilled champagne sits in a bucket on a low marble table, three lipstick-rimmed glasses filled with bubbles and honey-hued liquid.

Three bodies move on the large bed, the hungry sounds of skin slapping on skin something I've become acutely accustomed to over the past three days, not to mention all of my previous visits to parties like this. I clear my throat, hoping to get their attention. There are three girls, probably in their early twenties. They're all giggly and frothy from the champagne, and I wonder if their little party will extend to male company, or if it'll stay just these three.

"Three?" I ask, a little louder than is probably polite for this kind of thing.

Five minutes later, the girls are lined up on their knees in a neat row in front of the bed, their mouths open, their pink tongues ready. I would crack a joke about how this looks, but I'm kind of in a hurry, with at least fifteen more customers to attend to in this one place alone. I've got a list of parties to go to, some over here in Oakland, others in the city, and every-body wants their dose of the good stuff before the party fizzles out. If I were an enterprising drug manufacturer I'd have staff to deliver the other doses for me, but I don't trust anyone with my particular brand of magic.

Hence the naked girls. I place a pill on the tongue of the first one and watch her swallow it, checking her mouth and under her tongue, before offering her a champagne flute to wash down the chalky pill. She accepts, drinking the entire glass. I switch my focus to the second girl, repeating my actions, making certain that she swallows the pill.

The third girl is more coy than her friends, the introvert of the threesome. She looks at the red heart-shaped pill in my thumb and forefinger with apprehension. "I'll take it later," she says, crossing her arms over her breasts. I raise my eyebrows, taking my leather jacket off and offering it to her. Some people are just too damn inhibited to have a strange, tattoo-covered punk shove a pill down their throat while they're completely naked and on their knees. I get it. But also, she's not keeping my fucking pill to give to some asshole who will copy the formula I painstak-ingly created.

"It's now or never, princess," I say, holding the tablet up in the dim light. "There's zero harm in saying no. Honestly."

She stares at the pill, seemingly fascinated. "I

have a really strong gag reflex," she confesses. "If you put your finger on my tongue, I'll throw up."

I feel for her boyfriend, if she has one. Then again, perhaps that's why she's locked in a private room inside a sex club with two other women, no dicks to be seen. Except mine, and it'll be staying firmly inside my pants for the duration of the evening, and probably another couple of days as I recover from my case of Rosaline chafe.

I coach the girl to catch the pill in her throat by tilting her head back, and she takes it like a champ, gag reflex thankfully not affected. After she's swallowed, and sank half a bottle of champagne as a chaser, I sit on a sleek mustard-colored sofa in the corner of the room, and set my watch for thirty minutes. My cash is already downstairs, the next room ready for me. The girls go back to whatever it was they were doing on the bed, and I watch idly. I can think of worse things to be doing.

My phone vibrates nineteen minutes in. It's Merc.

She says it was Ty Capulet who wanted her to take your pills.

Huh. Fucking figures that one of those pricks would want to take away the one good thing I've got going for me. Fucking figures.

Rage boils up in me at the mention of that soul-sucking family. They're the kind of people who would climb over your dying body to take your last dollar, and they'd make sure to stand on your throat and finish you off while they were at it. The Capulets used to be like family, until they destroyed my family and scattered us to a dozen different corners of the globe. I'm the only one stubborn enough to stay in the ruined mansion that my trust fund owns, the only asset to any of our names anymore, a vestige of broken lives and ash and now, Rosaline's blood. Fucking bitch. I didn't know she was in with the Capulets. I never would have hooked up with her if I'd known. Now, I'm just glad I figured out what she was trying to steal before she managed to get away with it.

I hope it took a lot of torture to get that information out of her, but Rosaline is a coward. I bet she flipped on Ty before I even got to this party.

Any idea where this little shit is? I fire back. Three dots appear immediately.

He'll be at the birthday party tonight. In the city. You know, all that bullshit where they hand over the reins, or sell the cow, or whatever.

That's tonight. *Jesus*.

Something akin to jealousy ripples through me like fire, as I think of Avery Capulet getting engaged tonight.

I find it ironic as fuck that when we were tiny children, our parents had arranged for us to be married one day. Yeah. Me, a Montague, and Avery, the diamond in the Capulet family's crown.

Guess you can see how that turned out.

When? Exactly where? I type back to Merc.

Palatial Hotel. From 8pm on. You know which one he is?

I think back to the last time I say Ty Capulet, the little prick, after he testified against me in court and helped to send me to prison for two fucking years for something *he* did.

Yeah, I text back. I know exactly which one.

Dude. Wear a mask or something. They'll never let you near that place. You don't exactly blend.

I catch my reflection in the mirrored coffee table I'm hunched over and have to agree. My tattoos are pretty fucking conspicuous. The Montague crest on my back might be covered, but there's plenty more black and red ink snaking up my arms, all the way to my fingertips. Up my neck. Everywhere. Plus the small matter of me looking exactly, irredeemably like my exiled father, who is the only person more hated than me in this little criminal society in San Francisco.

I gave Rosaline something to knock her out. I'm meeting you there. You're not going in to their lair alone.

I smirk. **Swell,** I text back. **See you there.**

Somebody is going to get fucked up tonight, and not in a fun way, like these three giggling girls, whose doses of my special recipe have started to hit them. I wait eleven painstaking minutes, the entire time imagining exactly how I'll rearrange Ty Capulet's face.

That fucking family. They're like blood-sucking demons. Ghouls. They've taken everything from my family, and now one of them is trying to undermine me and steal my drug.

Haven't they taken enough?

Game on, motherfucker. You just messed with the wrong Montague.

I stalk to my car once I know my pills are safely dissolved in these girls' stomachs. When I get to my car, I open the door so hard I nearly wrench it off the fucking hinges. I wish I had a faster car, to rage-drive back to the city and smash right into the front doors of the Palatial Hotel, maybe take out some Capulet family members on my smash and grab mission. I intend to make an example of that family. A bloody one. And it might just involve taking their beloved princess Avery down a couple of notches.

When I finally get to the financial district in the city, I park in a handicapped spot — if I'm going to beat some people to a bloody pulp, may as well start breaking the rules now — and collect my supplies from the trunk of the Prius. Knife? Check. Something to cover my face? Check. Guns? Check and check.

The cells of fury that continue to multiply like cancer inside of my body propel me to the front entrance of the hotel. Before I get there, though, I hear screaming. Sirens. People start bursting out of the front of the hotel, spilling like bees from a hive that's crashed to the ground. They all look rich, and beautiful, and frightened as fuck.

How interesting.

Meet me round back, Merc texts me.

I change my trajectory, continuing down the edge of the building as people rush by, too panicked to even notice the enemy going for an evening stroll beside them. I round the side of the building, stepping into the shadows of the Palatial Hotel's loading dock, and that's when it seems that the universe is finally deciding to throw me a bone. A bone that looks like Avery fucking Capulet, stepping out of the service elevator, surrounded by security and clutching at some tall dude in a suit who looks like he'd eat her alive, given half a chance.

Hello, little lover. It's time your family was taught a lesson.

CHAPTER SEVEN

AVERY

*A*fter my father's speech, and then Joshua's, during which I stand beside him and smile and blink my pretty fake eyelashes and try to ignore the blisters forming from my new Manolo Blahniks; the party moves outside to the rooftop deck. There are thousands of tiny fairy lights strung over the massive pool, everything sparkling and shiny. Normally I would love being here, but tonight I just want to rip the shoes off my feet, tear off this ridiculous dress, and put on some pajamas. I've been instructed by my father that I have to stay until at least midnight — maybe longer, if I don't turn into a pumpkin — so I grab the prettiest drink from the nearest silver tray and try to appear semi-elegant while tipping it down my throat. The champagne bubbles tickle my nose and burn their way down my throat; but after a second flute, tossed back much the same way, a pleasant buzz filters through my veins and loosens my tense limbs. I'm reaching for a third glass when a hand presses against the small of my back, making me jump. I drop the champagne flute to the floor, where it shatters into a million tiny shards, tiny droplets of frothy liquid hitting my ankles. Fuck's sake.

I turn around, expecting Joshua, letting my shoulders drop in relief when I see my cousin and uncle both standing in front of me.

"Hey," I say to both of them, my tongue feeling a little thick in my mouth.

"Are you drunk?" Enzo asks, looking equal parts horrified and amused.

Nathan scowls. "Every damn time, I tell you. You have got to eat at these things."

I shrug, mostly sad that I don't have a fresh drink in my hand. "I'm not drunk," I protest. "Tipsy, but not drunk."

My uncle blinks slowly, as if in deep thought. "Maybe you should take Avery to freshen up, maybe have a snack?" Enzo suggests to Nathan, who nods in response.

"You want to cut out for a little while?" Nathan asks me, hugging me just long enough to bend down and murmur those words into my ear. I nod, and he grabs my hand, making a beeline for the exit.

I scan the crowd, looking to see if Joshua notices my exit. He appears oblivious, deep in discussion with my father, both of them laughing and sipping on amber-colored liquid in thick crystal tumblers. Well. I suppose I shouldn't be surprised that he's already moving on to business, but really? We've been engaged for literally thirty minutes.

Perhaps this is a good omen amongst the shitty day I've endured. Maybe he'll leave me well enough alone and treat this like a business arrangement after all.

Just as I'm crossing the threshold into the ball-room, Joshua meets my gaze. I stop in my tracks, my entire body freezing up. He grins, raising his glass, giving me a wink that makes me want to run over there and rip his fucking face off in front of everyone.

He must see my clear lack of enthusiasm, because his grin turns to an amused smirk, as he turns his attention back to my father and whatever they were talking about. I try to ignore the anger that wells up inside my chest as Nathan tugs my wrist gently.

I follow, my thoughts messy, my head pounding. We cross the ballroom, empty now save for a few stragglers, and Nathan scans his access card for the private elevator in the corridor.

Five minutes later, we're walking in to a sub-penthouse suite on the floor below where the party is being held. Relief floods my limbs immediately at the prospect of being alone and unencumbered for at least a few moments. I enter the room, flop down on the bed, and contemplate whether it's worth removing my shoes, only to have to put them back on again soon. I decide to leave them on, reclining against cool, fluffy pillows and stiff cotton sheets, the ache in my head still a constant throb. I close my eyes, wishing I could end the night here, wishing I didn't have to go back out there and be with him.

Nathan makes a tutting sound, turning all of the lights on in the room. It's suddenly unbearably bright, and I shield my eyes with my hand in protest. "Don't pike out on me yet, Aves," Nathan says, producing a bottle of whiskey from nowhere, pouring liquid into two ice-filled tumblers. "Here, get some of this into you."

I accept one of the glasses gratefully, suddenly having a flashback to when I was in Daddy's office earlier. Christ, no wonder I feel like shit. I've been drinking on and off since midday - and that doesn't even include the pot I smoked with Nathan before I went to break up with Will.

Will. I wonder where he is now. The way things ended was beyond awful. I need to call him later, try to smooth things over, if that's even possible. I have no idea if he'll ever want to speak to me again.

I take one sniff of the straight whiskey Nathan's handed me, and my stomach roils. Oh, shit. The three glasses of champagne I pounded have all hit me at once, and I blink, suddenly dizzy and nauseous.

"You look green," Nathan says.

Bile rushes up my throat and I barely make it to the bathroom in time to throw up in the sink. *Eughhhhh.* Salt water bites at the corners of my eyes as I choke on my own vomit, my head buzzing angrily.

Two more heaves and my stomach settles. I grimace, turning the cold water on full, letting it wash away the entirely liquid diet I've consumed today. I wipe my mouth with a towel, searching for one of those tiny tubes of complimentary toothpaste that every bathroom in the Palatial should have. *Bingo.* I find the tube on a shelf beside the basin and rip the cap off, squeezing toothpaste directly into my mouth and swishing it around. Better. I'm minty fresh again, and nobody will ever know that I just puked my guts up in a moment where I should be poised and regal.

Except I look like garbage. I study myself in the mirror. I need to reapply my foundation, get some eyedrops for my bloodshot eyes, and fix the smudged eyeliner under my left eye. I have nothing on me — not a purse, not a phone. "Hey, Nathan?" I call into the room.

He appears in the bathroom doorway, looking worried. "I told you to eat something," he admonishes, bringing his hand up to my cheek and using his thumb to wipe under my eye. "You want me to grab you something?"

I teeter on my heels, no longer nauseous, but still drunk. "Yes please," I say sweetly. "And hey, Nath, can you see if you can find Jennifer? She has all of my makeup in her purse."

Nathan nods, disappearing. I hear the soft click of the door closing, and turn off all of the lights, making a beeline for the bed. I'll take a micro nap while Nathan's gone. I close my eyes, and I'm unconscious before my head even hits the pillow.

I don't know how long I sleep — it could be three seconds or three hours — but I wake suddenly, uneasily, a loud noise puncturing my dreamless void. I sit up with a start, my head reeling as I search in the dark for the switch on the lamp next to the bed. For a moment I don't even remember where I am.

Hotel room. Vomit. Nathan going to get me food.

Right.

It takes me a moment to piece together what the noise was that woke me. The hotel room door, slamming shut. They normally have a soft closing mechanism, so whoever slammed it had to use a fair amount of force. Suddenly, my inebriation lifts, and I'm on high alert.

Without warning, a hand jerks out, pulling me upright. I squeal, but a hand is immediately placed over my mouth.

"Shh. Be quiet," a male voice murmurs.

The lamp beside me snaps on and I get a good look at the person who's just scared the living shit out of me.

"Will?" I say in disbelief. "What the hell are you doing here?"

Will looks disheveled. His hair is messy, his dress shirt is wrinkled. And he smells of booze. *Pot, meet kettle.*

"I'm here to save you," Will says. *Oh, shit.*

"Oh my God," I whisper. "Are you for real? Will, we spoke about this."

"Yeah. I know," he says, as I try to gauge how

drunk he is. "We've been speaking about this for eight years."

"We can still see each other," I say. "But things will have to be different now."

"Yeah. I got the memo about that," he snaps. "Thanks. You know what they're doing to you isn't fair. It's probably even illegal."

I throw my hands up in frustration. "There's nothing I can do about it now." I point at the engagement ring on my left finger to illustrate my point.

Will grabs both of my hands and squeezes a little too hard. It's almost painful. "Yes, there *is* something you can do about it," he hisses. "Something we can both do about it. My father's jet is fueled up and ready to go wherever you want, Avery. We can go away from all this. It's not like any law enforcement in the world would ever look at this situation and think that you need to be transported back to your fucked up family."

Oh my God, he wants me to run away with him? "Where would we go?" I ask slowly. I don't know why I ask that, because there's no way in hell I'm going anywhere. I'm really just stalling for time, waiting for Nathan to get back with my food and my best friend and my makeup. "Will—"

"Just stop, Avery," he cuts me off. "Just stop

thinking about your family for once. Stop thinking about your obligations. Stop chasing your father around like if you do what he says he'll start giving a fuck about you! The only person Augustus Capulet thinks about is Augustus Capulet. So think about yourself for once, Avery. Think about *me*."

"I can't," I say. "I'm sorry."

He drops my hands, a look of resignation on his face. "So, what, that's it? You're just going to go out there, with this engagement ring on. Marry that fucking guy who's been stalking you since you were a child?"

"Since I was sixteen," I say.

"Exactly. Sixteen. TEEN. And the only reason you met him in the first place was because he was lined up to marry your sister."

"I know that," I say. "Do you think I haven't thought about this before, Will? About running away?"

"So do it," he urges. "Come away with me. We'll go somewhere tropical. Somewhere where there are umbrellas in every drink. Somewhere far away from California where we can have a real life."

"We won't have any money," I whisper. "I might have a massive trust fund, but do you think I'll be able to access even one penny of it if I run away from all of this?"

Will shakes his head. "*I* have money, plenty of money. Look, it's not Capulet money, but my father isn't exactly poor, you know. And unlike *your* father, he's not a fucking idiot who wants me to marry some asshole for a business deal."

I feel sick again. I need to lie down. I need to run away, but I don't need to run away from my family. I need to run away from Will, even though what he's saying makes perfect sense, even though I should take his hand and walk out of here and never look back. But I can't — I'm like a child who's been raised in a cult. My devotion to my family, however reluctant, eclipses the love I have for Will. For anybody. And that's the worst part in all of this. I won't go against my father, because I am so greedy for his approval, so desperate for the love he dishes out in measured doses, even though what he's doing to my life is unforgivable.

"I'm sorry, Will," I say. "There's nothing stopping us from seeing each other, just like we have been. We'll just have to be discreet."

Will swipes the lamp on the bedside table to the ground with ferocity, and speed. It falls over, smashing. I flinch at the sound. It's not the first lamp he's broken in my presence. Will has broken plenty of things in the years I've known him. Lamps. Noses. Windows. His emotions run hot, always on the surface, constantly threatening to boil over and burn everything in its wake. I've never been afraid of him doing something to me, but I've been terrified of what he might do to someone else more times than I can count. Sometimes, passion comes at a price.

"You were never going to choose me," he spits. "Even if your father had allowed it. I've waited for you all this time, Avery. I moved my whole life to San Francisco. I left my friends. I left my family. For fucks sake, I got myself legally emancipated to come here for you, because I *love* you. I fucking love you! And now you're telling me that I'm just going to be your afternoon delight whenever it suits you and your *husband*?"

"Don't say it like that," I protest. "*All* I want is to be with you."

"But it *is* like that. When I pictured our future, I was thinking a wedding. I was thinking of having a family. Normal things that people do. Do you really expect me to just hang around in the shadows while you go off and *fuck* this guy and share *his* bed and have *his* children? Really? Because let me tell you,

Avery Capulet — I'm nobody's patsy. I'm nobody's fool."

"No," I say. "I don't expect you to hang around in the shadows."

"Right," he replies. "So it's like that. Okay. Fine. I'll see myself out, shall I?"

His calm is false, and it's even more terrifying than his violence.

"Will, please, don't do anything stupid."

"The only one doing anything *stupid* here is you, Avery. You think this will solve everything, doing what that man says? *How high should I jump this time, Daddy? Which man should I fuck this week, Daddy?* Putting that stupid fucking ring on? So heavy it's probably going to break your hand? It looks ridiculous."

I swallow uneasily, his words stinging barbs. "I have a responsibility to this family."

"Bullshit, you do." He grabs my shoulders, yanking me forward so that our noses are almost touching. "You have a responsibility to me, Avery. I gave you eight years of my life. *I want them back.*"

"You're scaring me," I say quietly.

Anger flares in his eyes. "I'm scaring you?" He draws his fist back and punches the wall next to the bed, making me flinch.

"You should be scared," Will rages. "You should be terrified. Because if you think I'm going to take this shit laying down, baby, you don't know me at all."

He throws me back against the pillows violently, where I stay, frozen, watching as he storms out of the room. The door slams again, and I'm alone.

CHAPTER EIGHT

AVERY

I return to the party a little while later, after some aspirin and a hefty pile of miniature cheeseburgers that were being served to the guests. Jennifer, my best friend since we were little girls, takes great care with fixing my makeup and neatening my hair, while Nathan feeds me little sips of cherry Gatorade.

I don't tell either of them what happened with Will. I'm going to pretend it was a bad dream for now, until I can process what he said in the light of day. As it is, what he said — me stealing years of his life — is a cancerous guilt that is slowly making it's way through my body, settling in my stomach like a lead weight. I'm pretty good at compartmentalizing things in general — I've had plenty of practice, after all — but something about his anger, the raw desperation in his eyes, has rattled me.

Luckily, my delightful new fiancé is around to snap me out of any uneasy daydreams my mind is spinning about Will.

"Avery, darling," Joshua says, giving me a look that says *Where the fuck have you been*, as he wraps a hand around my waist and pulls me in. "I'd like you to meet some people."

I groan inwardly, plastering a smile on my freshly-glossed lips. "Show the way, lover," I reply with a fake sweetness, one that contains a deadly venom bite. I spend the next little while shaking hands with people whose names I will not remember, whose small talk I couldn't give a fuck about, nursing a champagne flute without drinking any.

"You don't like your drink?" Joshua asks, steering me into a quiet corner as people start to get loose and loud around us. "I can get you anything you like."

"Gee, thanks honey," I reply. "Can you get me another fiancé? One of my own choosing?"

Joshua laughs, my insults barely registering on his radar. "Isn't that the guy who was in your room before? Will Hewitt? I thought for sure you'd take his offer and frolic off into the sunset with him."

I feel my mouth drop open.

"Oh come on, Avery. You're not the only one who knows your way around this hotel. I own a minority stake in the Palatial, remember?"

"Right," I say. "That's why you're always creeping around here."

He pulls a face, tucking a stray hair behind my ear. "Let's be real. You're the only reason I creep around here, sweetheart." He gestures to the crowd. "To be honest, I was starting to lose hope that this would ever happen. Your father has been incredibly patient with your desires to experience a career and have a relationship before you finally settled down to your real job."

Ugh. He didn't. "My real job?"

He takes the flute of warm champagne from my hand and places it on the table beside him. "Avery, you've got a multi-billion dollar company to run. Not to mention, a bunch of Capulet babies to make. I know you're young, but don't worry — that's what I'm here for."

"Thank you, my prince," I reply, my words dripping with sarcasm. "I don't know what I'd do without you."

Joshua smiles at me as if I'm a petulant child stamping her foot. "You're so pretty when you're angry," he says. "I know you think your ice queen act is protecting you from me, but I've always liked the cold."

I open my mouth to respond, but I never get the chance. A loud bang echoes in the night, and everyone still on the outside deck draws in a collective gasp.

Joshua's hand wraps around my wrist as he jerks me into his side. For once I'm not trying to stop him — I'm craning my neck, searching for the origin of the noise, or at least the damage. The first thing that comes to mind is *It's probably just fireworks*. The second is *What the fuck has Will done?*

I get my answer soon enough. I scan the guests, but nobody seems to be hurt, just rattled. I check off my nearest and dearest — Nathan and Jennifer are standing beside the exit, seemingly oblivious as she tucks her blonde hair behind her ear and giggles at whatever story he's telling her. Uncle Enzo is at the bar that sits beside the far end of the pool, his hand outstretched and waiting for a fresh beverage. And my father is standing at a long table beside the pool that is groaning with food and champagne glasses, a few feet from Enzo, a strange expression on his face.

It's dark, but not dark enough that I don't see the

red spot on my father's white shirt. At first I dismiss it, thinking it's just the rose he had tucked in to his suit jacket earlier, but then I see the round spot spread across his shirt, getting wider.

"Daddy?" I yell across the pool. My father takes a faltering step toward the pool's edge, still on his feet, still looking completely fine apart from the red on his shirt and the strange, frozen expression on his face. He looks toward me, his glass falling from his hand in slow motion as he grabs for something to steady himself. He catches the end of the table with his hand, but it doesn't slow his trajectory forward, into the pool. I hear a scream as he hits the water's surface, and it takes me a second to realize the sound is coming from me.

The table full of food crashes into the pool a second later, tortilla chips and napkins scattering across the water's surface as a widening puddle of blood marks the spot where my father is rapidly sinking to the pool's bottom. People scream and flee, confusion in the herd, everyone trying to fit through the double doors that lead to the ballroom and beyond.

I watch in horror as Uncle Enzo jumps into the water fully clothed, followed immediately by Nathan.

I step toward the pool, intending to do the same thing myself, but a hand clamps around my wrist like a vise. I look down to see who is holding me back. Of course. My nightmare.

"Let go of me," I half-sob, wrenching my arm as hard as I can from Joshua's grip. He has moved from smirking asshole into overprotective fiancé in the space of approximately three seconds, wrapping his arm around my shoulders and ferrying me toward the exit. "Let go of me!" I scream. He releases his grip momentarily, and I rush to the edge of the pool just in time to see Enzo bring my father to the edge of the pool. Nathan is already out, soaked from head to toe, and he's crouched at the edge of the pool, his arms hooking under neath my father's arms and pulling.

I kneel beside him, reaching out to help, when Nathan notices me. "Get out of here!" he yells, water like a river down his face. "Josh! Get her inside!"

"No," I protest, as Joshua pulls me up and starts dragging me to the exit, where Jennifer is standing with a shocked expression on her face. "No!"

Joshua, his resolve apparently strengthened by Nathan's demand, corrals me through the exit. I notice several security guards gather around us as we move, their movements choreographed and swift. They all have guns drawn, all wearing black suits, every one of them with earpieces in their ear. I continue to struggle with Joshua, anxiety pumping through my veins like some kind of adrenalin overdose, my thoughts locked on one objective: to get back to my father. To make sure he's OK. *Is he dead? Will he die before I can get back to him? Is somebody calling an ambulance? Why can't I hear sirens?*

"Avery, stop," Joshua snaps. He pushes me into the wall of the narrow corridor that leads to our private Capulet elevator, the security guards still a tight circle around us. But nobody interferes. They're like a wall of muscle separating us from the rest of the world, human shields, but none of them are going to tell Joshua not to manhandle me to shut me up.

"Is he okay?" I gasp, my entire body ice-cold. "Is he dead?"

I'm still fighting Joshua's grip, his fingernails digging into me.

"Hey!" Joshua yells, shaking me hard enough that there'll be bruises on my arms tomorrow. "He's not dead, but you might be if you don't stop fighting me. Look at me, damnit!"

And then his hands are holding my jaw, his grip unforgiving. He forces me to look up at him, tilts my chin up and forces me to stay like that while he speaks fevered words to me.

"Someone just put a bullet in your father, who do you think they'll be aiming for next?" he snaps, looking out of his mind with worry. He lets go of me, stepping back and running a hand through his hair absently. "You stupid girl. Do you want to get shot, too?"

I do not want to get shot.

"Do you?" he presses.

I shake my head, thankful for the slap for pulling me out of my daze. "No."

He points down the hall. "Then get in the *goddamn* elevator."

I push off the wall, teetering on trembling legs. Joshua reaches out to steady me, and this time, I don't try to push him away. It might be a small victory that he's won over me already, but I don't think he's keeping score right now. His smarmy mask has slipped off, and his singular focus right now is getting both of us to safety.

Which, as terrible as it seems, is actually kind of a comfort. Because I don't need anyone as much as my father needs to be surrounded by family members. Enzo and Nathan being with him, and Jennifer nearby, gives me a great measure of comfort that if he dies, he won't die alone. I hope they're holding his hand. I hope someone is comforting him and whispering in his ear that everything will be okay, that help is coming. These are the thoughts crawling around in my panicked mind like half-trampled cockroaches as Joshua and I stand in the middle of a tight circle of security guards, in an elevator large enough for the comfort of only one or two people, but weight-capable of many more, designed for situations just like this. I know the drill. Much the same way as school children are taught to clamber into bathrooms and under desks in the event of an emergency, so have I been taught what to do in situations such as this. I know before the doors open that we will be on the ground floor, in the loading dock. I know that there will be a car waiting to whisk us away, more security guards, the city's traffic on lockdown from the moment the alarm is raised to allow us a quick exit.

The doors open, and two of the security guards leave the lift, moving forward into the dark loading area, guns drawn. There is a sleek black limousine sitting in the middle of the otherwise empty loading area, a standard security inclusion for events such as tonight's. The guards motion for us to come out, and that's when the shit really hits the fan. As soon as all of us are out of the lift and its doors are closed, a man steps out of the shadows, seemingly from nowhere, a balaclava covering his face. He raises his arm, a series of muted pops followed swiftly by the security guards dropping like flies. Joshua pulls me in to him protectively — such a stand-up guy — his eyes bugging out as the balaclava-wearing assassin steps forward, yanking me away as he presses a taser into the crook of Joshua's neck.

My fiancé goes down like a sack of shit, his entire body spasming as he lands unceremoniously at my feet.

Fuck! In the space of less than ten seconds, this guy has picked off six security guards who are ex-marines and highly trained mercenaries, and not one of them is moving. *How is this happening?* I back up, turning to run for the lift, but I don't find the smooth metal of the lift doors that I'm expecting. Instead, I smack straight into a hard chest. *There are two of them.* That's how they shot everyone so fast. Leather-gloved hands wrap around my wrists, bile burning in my throat as I tip my head back, looking up at this faceless man, taking in any identifying detail that I can find on my second assassin — who, ironically, is dressed exactly the same as the first one. Black clothes, black balaclavas, black leather gloves, black motorcycle boots. This man — or his accomplice — could literally be my own father and I wouldn't be able to tell. Except, I know it's not my father, because my father is bleeding to death on the roof of the building.

"Please," I beg, the weight of my mortality like an anchor dragging me underwater. It's all-consuming, this despair, the way I can't stop my entire body from shaking with terror, the pain from the hands squeezing my wrists to breaking point. He spins me in his arms, too easily, so that my back is against his chest. He's a whole head taller than me and then some, and his chin digs into the top of my scalp so I can't even turn my head.

The first guy — the one I saw when the guards started toppling like dominoes — lunges forward, his gun nowhere to be seen. The one behind me pushes me forward roughly, and the one in front shoves something over my face. It's a black bag, that feels like rough calico, and smells like pennies and leather. I open my mouth to scream, but the noise morphs into a strangled howl as something sharp stabs into the top of my arm. My suspicion that I've been injected with something is confirmed when a searing pain spreads across my bicep and down my arm, making my fingers go numb.

Jesus. What did they give me? It fucking hurts. Whatever it is, I don't have too long to contemplate it's origins, because the world outside my covered face goes quiet, sounds zooming in and out of my consciousness, my limbs softening like butter left out in the sun, until it's as if someone has simply switched me off and sent me into a black, endless void.

CHAPTER NINE

AVERY

I slowly come to, and then I'm awake all at once. Awake, alone, and completely blind.

Is the bag still over my head? I wriggle around a little, trying to figure out where I am, where my limbs have gone, why I'm so slow to piece together my thoughts.

Drugs. I remember the sharp pain of a needle jabbing in to my arm, the burn that spread through my veins once whatever I was injected with began to move through my body like wildfire.

Somebody gave me something.

It knocked me the fuck out. Everything buzzed, and then shorted out. I have no idea how long I've been unconscious. Where was I? What was I doing? What was being done to me?

My thoughts are soggy, heavy, weighted down by the drugs. I tug at my arms again. Where are my goddamn *arms*? More feeling comes to me, in tiny increments.

I'm on a chair.

Wait. I'm *tied* to the chair.

I try to twist my wrists out of whatever bindings they're in, and I feel the tiny hairs on my arms protest.

Tape. Whoever it was used tape.

Where are my legs? I can't feel them. There's only a numb buzz below my waist. I concentrate as much as I can through my haze, straining at the same time to hear anything that might indicate where I am, and if there's anyone else near me.

Where. Am I?

Then it comes rushing in, like ice water has been poured over me. *They shot my father.* A single gunshot that cracked everything apart. My father, in his tuxedo, dropping his whiskey on hard tiles, the glass exploding at his feet as blood blossomed across his white dress shirt. His trajectory into the pool, the heavy splash of his dead weight as five hundred people in ballgowns and designer suits screamed and scattered, nobody wanting to be gunshot victim number two. My desire to jump into the water after my uncle, to help him save my dad. The hands that clamped around my arms hard enough to cause bruises, as Joshua and my own personal security team whisked me away, to supposed safety, and straight into a trap.

Somebody shot my father *just so they could take me*. As a diversion. And they didn't fuck around. I saw where they shot him — right in the middle of his chest.

Is he even alive to know that I've been stolen away?

"What do you want?" I finally ask the darkness that presses against every edge of me. My throat hurts when I speak, thirst piercing my voice and turning it into a rasp. How long have I been here?

Where is here?

My blindfold is thick, but soft, like silk. Maybe several layers of silk.

"My family will pay whatever ransom you want," I say.

"Just tell them what you want. They'll give it to you."

I don't even know if there is anyone with me.

Anyone watching me.

I could be buried alive, or in somebody's attic, or in my own fucking house. I can't see. *I don't know.*

Fear continues to drip into my veins like poison. Behind the fear, the remains of my Capulet pride: *Who on earth would be stupid enough to take Augustus Capulet's daughter from him?*

"Listen," I say, trying to be convincing, which is hard when I'm tied to a chair, my wrists and ankles secured with what feels like duct tape, the blindfold tied tight around my face. "Just tell me—"

What feels like a large, rough palm smacks me so hard, I feel my lip split, taste the copper of fresh blood on my mouth. I let out a wail. I've never been so terrified in my life — I was so sure that I was talking to thin air. How long has this person been in front of me, waiting for me to wake up?

My mind struggles to catch up, to do something — but before I can think, before I can construct the perfect argument to *let me go*, my blindfold is ripped off, and in the same breath, shoved into my mouth. A makeshift gag that makes me retch. I swallow down the urge to vomit, the material in my mouth an invasion, an assault on my senses. My eyes are twin orbs of lancing pain at the sudden weak light that hits them, as I try to decipher my surroundings now that I have sight. The gag irritates my throat, and I try to push it out with my tongue, but it doesn't budge.

Fuck. *Oh fuck oh fuck oh fuck.* I forget about the gag as my eyes focus on the figure in front of me. He's tall, over six feet, dressed entirely in black, the same black ski mask from earlier over his head. He's wearing plastic surgical gloves now, the leather ones nowhere to be seen — to keep his DNA from getting on me, or in preparation to chop me into little pieces?

I glance down at myself. The bottom half of my dress is gone, the puffy gauze skirt a remnant of a night long left behind. It sits in a heap of tulle in one corner of this room I'm in, which I can now see is about the size of a large bedroom, the floor made of rough concrete. I can see a thin mattress against one wall of the room, a small dining table on the other. There's a large, horizontal mirror that takes up almost one entire wall of the room, and beside it, a metal door that looks thick and heavy. *That's my escape route*, I think, filing that information away for another time. I steal little glances around, trying to learn as much as I can about where I am, but at the same time never taking my attention away from the man in front of me.

The room is lit only by a single blue lamp on a table in the corner, the shadows in here long and menacing against the blank, grey cement walls. My captor reaches for something on the table, and I crane my neck to see what he's holding.

A knife.

I start to hyperventilate, which is kind of fucking hard to do when you only have your nose to breathe through. He brings the knife up to my belly and rests it right between my breasts, still wrapped in the top half of the dress that I was sewn into just hours ago. Or was it longer than just a few hours ago? How long have I been down here?

It can't have been that long, I think. My bladder is uncomfortably full, but not painful, yet — so it can't have been more than a few hours that I've been here. I've not used a toilet that I can remember, and my underwear doesn't feel wet. So by those calculations, it's probably the early hours of the morning.

I recoil, squeezing my eyes shut as balaclava guy cuts my dress corset clear down the middle, yanking the material away from my body with a desperation that almost borders on hunger. My breasts bounce free from the once-tight material, my nipples immediately stiffening to hard peaks against the bitter chill in this tiny room. The dress corset had a bra built into it, so cutting it away leaves me naked from the waist up. All I have on now are my plain flesh-colored panties, seamless at the edges so that my dress sat properly, without a panty line. Even those are taken from me, the knife nicking the material at each of my hips so that the material falls away. My legs are parted slightly on the chair, and the cold air reaches inside my thighs, pulling a painful sigh from me that nobody will ever hear. My knees are shaking so badly against the cold, it's a wonder I don't make the chair topple onto its side, and me with it.

I wince as my captor places something cold on my bare thigh. *The knife.* I protest through the gag in my mouth, nothing but a garbled, muted noise filtering through the material. I'm naked, I'm begging, I'm shaking, I'm fucking sobbing, but he doesn't pay my pleas the slightest bit of attention. My eyes go big and round as I watch him take that knife and press it into the flesh of my inner thigh. The pain is so hot, so acidic, that vomit rushes up my throat. I choke it back down with great difficulty, my nose burning with the sudden rush of bile that would have probably poured out of my nose if I hadn't swallowed it back down. I stare at the burgeoning wound being sawn into my thigh, as if I'm a patient who's just sat up in the middle of a major surgery and seen inside herself.

There is a major artery that runs through the inside of the thigh. I remember from biology class.

What's it called? If he hits it, I could bleed out in minutes.

Just hours ago, I was joking about how being married off was a fate worse than death. But I didn't really mean those words, because I'd do anything to stop the slow, methodical slice of the knife's teeth against my skin. I scream as my skin splits open, the knife impossibly sharp, my skin impossibly fragile. I stare down at the spot on my own body where a neat red line appears, and then starts to spill out like the water that gushes over the edge of a waterfall. There is *so much blood.* I've seen plenty of blood spilled in my short life — a by-product of my family name — but I've never been so intimately acquainted with my own blood as it pulses from my body. I'm unbearably cold, my teeth chattering. I have no idea if it's actually cold in here or if it's because I'm losing so much blood, so quickly, but either way, I'm so cold that every bit of exposed skin on my body breaks out in gooseflesh.

My captor dips a finger into my blood and brings it up to my chest. I'm folding forward, straining to see what he's doing to my thigh, and so he takes a fistful of my hair and yanks, making me sit straighter in the chair. I shiver as the air in the room turns colder, my exposed nipples tightening painfully, or perhaps it's me that is growing colder, as I swiftly lose blood.

Fingers paint letters between my breasts, a macabre action that reminds me of the crude paintings a small child would create with their hands and brightly colored paint. My faceless captor takes blood from my thigh wound several more times before he steps back, apparently satisfied, and it's only then that I can see what he's written on me.

Two letters. **XO.**

I blink in confusion as I stare at the two letters, my chin against my chest as I try to make them say something — anything — else. Everybody knows the XO killer doesn't have any surviving victims. He only leaves death in his wake, naked and scrubbed clean and with a neat calling card painted on his victims' chests.

*X*o.

*I*t's so obvious now. He doesn't want a ransom. He wants my terror. He wants my *life*.

This silent psycho circles behind me, hands in my

hair again, and then lower, exploring my face, my neck, pinching a nipple hard enough to make me yelp. He pulls my hair, forcing my head back and to the side, at the perfect height to grind his erection into my cheek. Under his black pants, he's as hard as the steel the knife is forged from. I start to cry. He's going to hurt me.

He's going to murder me.

I raise my eyes to look at him again, in time to see him place the knife on the ground at his feet. My captor comes at me, crouching in front of me, placing his gloved hands on my knees and pushing them wider. Without the pressure of my other thigh, my wound bleeds faster, more urgently, as I struggle to get enough air through my nose. He takes one glove off, making a show of trailing the limp plastic across my skin, throwing it to the ground as he aims his index finger toward my vagina and pushes in. I groan through my gag in protest, the breach of my most private place horrific, his finger large and rough and trying to push somewhere with zero lubrication. I tighten up every muscle involuntarily, wanting to keep him out, wanting to fold in on myself and die right here before he can molest me any more.

The resistance frustrates him, I can tell. He stops trying to finger-fuck an unwilling orifice and turns his attention back to my thigh. He pushes his fingers into the cut he's made in my thigh, and a muffled groan tries to fight its way through my gag. Sharp white pain rings clear all around me as the damaged nerves in my leg scream for mercy. He uses his blood-slicked fingers to breach me again, and this time, he finds purchase. I'm impossibly tight down there, from fear and my body's desire to expel the painful intrusion, but all that does is tighten my walls around his finger as he pushes and pulls, in and out. His thumb finds my clitoris, nothing more than the gentlest brush over it's protective hood, but the motion causes my entire body to jump in response. He tips his head to the side, cupping my ass in his palm as he pulls me forward in the seat.

I scream again; but really, what's the use? Nobody will hear me. Nobody will help me. How would they? My ass is now right on the edge of the chair, the position causing the back of the chair to dig into the exact spot in my spine where I laid against the hard edge of the mausoleum alter less than twenty-four hours ago while Will drove himself inside me. Was that a different life? It feels so far away, so hard to grab onto the memory, but with every bite of the chair's hard edge into my back, the memory of being with Will sharpens.

Will. Where did you go? Are you looking for me?

A second, more sickening thought.

Were you a part of this? Is this your way of getting your life back?

No. He would *never.* No, the man kneeling between my legs as I slowly bleed to death on this chair is a stranger, of that I am sure. I have never been more sure of anything in my life. You couldn't know a person and subject them to this. You couldn't love somebody for eight years and then have any part in something so terrifyingly cruel, so deviant.

Just this morning I was lamenting my situation, cursed to bear the Capulet name, and now all I want to do is use my name and my power to free myself from this situation, this place, this man, his rough fingers.

And they're just his fingers, aren't they? I should be thankful that he's not trying to stick his dick in me. But I'm *not* grateful. I'm rocked to the core, literally, every push of his fingers, every scrape of his finger-nails inside me a brutal reality, a violent awakening.

*his is how I die.*

. . .

*T*hrough my gag, I scream.

*H*e slaps me again, hard enough to snap my head back with force. He raises himself from his spot on the ground, just high enough to pull the wet blindfold out of my mouth. He fixes it over my eyes, and I'm blind again, this time the saliva-slicked material sticking to my skin like glue. "Please," I beg him. There's a small gap in the bottom of the blindfold, and I hold my breath in horror as I watch him roll up the balaclava just enough to expose his chin and mouth. It's too dark to make out much detail, and I can only tell that he's clean-shaven. It's too dark to make out the shape of his jaw, the color of his skin, anything.

I can feel his hot breath drift over my thighs, as he pushes my knees wide and settles between my legs again, the sharp back of the chair making my back feel like it might break in half. I focus on the pain, though, a welcome distraction from what I fear he's about to do.

Please don't.

He does. He pushes and pushes at my knees, until it feels like my hips will snap, and he plants a long, lingering kiss right on my swollen bud of nerves. He kisses it like you would kiss somebody's mouth, his tongue massaging me in long, rolling waves, until I'm panting, until I'm no longer trying to pull away because all I'm doing is making more friction between his mouth and my skin, my energy spent, my limbs like lead weights. It feels dirty, this contact. It feels disgusting. It's something a lover does. Not the stranger who has taken you hostage.

"Help!" I scream. "Somebody! Help!"

He laughs against my clitoris, and the vibration only makes it worse. I would prefer to be beaten on the ground, to be tasered. Anything but this.

He pulls away, and then I feel fingers tugging at the rock on my hand. Of course. My gazillion-dollar engagement ring. What I'd give right now, to be the unhappy fiancé of Joshua Grayson, milling around my birthday party, making small talk.

What I'd give.

CHAPTER TEN

ELLIOT MCRAE

*Y*ou know it's going to be a shitty night when there aren't enough body bags to clean up all the dead people.

I'm standing in a loading dock underneath a hotel that sits on the edge of the financial district in San Francisco, trying to figure out what happened to all of these highly trained, ex-military guys to cause them to be dead and scattered all around me. Why somebody shot the owner of the building, and then snatched his daughter from under everyone's nose.

I'm also trying to figure out why *the fuck* my boss would put me on a case like this. It's high-profile — the Capulet family would normally be taken care of by senior ranking Federal Officers, not ones who, by rights, probably shouldn't even have a badge and gun.

Yet, here I am.

Three feet from me, I know my partner is probably feeling the same. It's an uneasy feeling, knowing that there's probably a fucked-up reason behind being assigned to a case you should be running from. But when the Director of the Federal Bureau of Investigations personally calls you at home on a Sunday night and tells you to get down to the Palatial Hotel to investigate the shooting murders of at least six people, a high-profile abduction, and the attempted murder of one of the most powerful men in California, you get your ass down to the crime scene, a-fucking-sap.

"This is a mess," Isobel Sazerac murmurs, stepping over a dead security guard to get to me. I nod at my fellow Detective in agreement. "It's a shit show, alright."

"We got what we need from here?" she asks.

I shrug. "I think we should leave Forensics to do their thing. Get some more statements before the rest of the guests find a way out of there." I point above me, to the ceiling, and beyond, where tired, frazzled party guests are starting to complain loudly and throw around words like *lawyer* and *civil rights*.

Truth be told, I want to get out of here as quickly as possible. I've seen my fair share of dead people, including some that met their end because of me, but this is different. The scent of blood is ripe on the night air, heavy and metallic, and death has always made me a little queasy. Not enough to stop doing what I do, but enough that I always manage to avoid attending the autopsies until the bodies are sewn back up and safely zipped back into their body bags.

We step away from the sea of bodies, conferring in a little alcove near the sidewalk outside the dock. The entire block has been cordoned off — no chance of press catching our conversation, what with the seemingly hundreds of SFPD officers forming an impenetrable wall around the Palatial Hotel building.

I take a proper look at Isobel; with her blow-dried brown tresses and heavily-lined blue eyes, she could pass for one of the party guests, not one of the FBI agents investigating the bloody aftermath of Augustus Capulet's shooting, and his daughter's disappearance.

"Were you asleep when they called, Grandpa?" Isobel asks, tipping her head to the side and studying my face.

"Were you pole dancing?" I reply. "'Because those sneakers don't exactly match your dress."

Isobel pulls a face. "I was on a hot date, actually."

"Oh. I was watching Frozen for the hundredth time."

Isobel blinks.

"With Kayla," I add.

Isobel pulls a notepad from her coat pocket. "Your daughter has excellent taste in Disney movies, then," she says, flipping the notepad open and handing it to me. I take it, scanning down a list of names.

"Which one do you think is the most suspicious?" she asks.

I read off each name before settling on one. "Will Hewitt would be my bet," I say. "Then again, Lorenzo Capulet stands to benefit if his brother doesn't make it."

Isobel shrugs. "That's what I thought, too, about the brother, right? Enzo, they call him. But apparently that's not how it works. I asked one of the cousins, a kid called Tyler?"

I nod for her to continue.

"As of tonight, Avery Capulet is the sole beneficiary of everything the Capulets own."

"Everything?" I echo. "Isn't that, like—"

"More money than you or I could ever fathom," Isobel says. "Which begs the question — why haven't they asked for a ransom yet?"

I shrug. "It's only been a couple hours. They probably want to scare them first, you know, beat her up a little bit, maybe figure out their demands?"

Isobel shakes her head. "What I don't get is —

she was apparently wearing an engagement ring worth eight million dollars. Eight. That's like, Beyoncé level. Why not just take the ring, dump her off a few blocks away, and high-tail it?"

We start walking toward the hotel foyer. "Maybe it's not about the money. Maybe it's something else they want with her, with the family."

Isobel shakes her head, taking the notepad back from me. "No way. With people like this, it's always about the money."

---

*W*e get statements from as many guests as we can, starting with the Capulet family members and spanning outward. The Will kid, Avery Capulet's freshly dumped ex-boyfriend, is distraught. Too distraught for me to think he's got anything to do with Avery's disappearance, unless he's an incredible actor. His old man has a wall of Academy Awards, so I make a mental note to look into the apple and see how far it fell from the tree. But actually, the one person in all of this who gives me the creeps is the fiancé. Joshua Grayson. I don't know what it is about him — maybe that he's the one who led her down to the dock? Or the fact that he was the only one to escape without a scratch, while six security officers were shot and killed in cold blood.

Then again, with her father on the brink of death, maybe the fiancé's just been kept alive to make sure the ransom gets paid.

Back at the FBI Headquarters, I make a beeline for the coffee machine. "Yes please," Isobel calls out, already knowing where I'm off to. It's almost three a.m., and we've both been on call since eight yesterday morning. I don't mind the long shifts, especially when the case is something as important as finding a missing girl, but I need caffeine to push through.

The coffee maker in our lunch room is one of those pod machines. I grab two mugs, heap sugar into them, and take two of the strongest pods, dropping one into the machine and selecting the largest shot of coffee. The machine roars to life, loud enough to wake the dead security guards who are by now probably en route to the city morgue. I watch as rich, brown coffee pours from the machine. *Huh.* It's the exact color of the missing girls' eyes. How does a girl go missing like that, in the middle of hundreds of people? At her own party, no less? Whoever snatched her was prepared, I know that much. I also know the coffee machine is being a temperamental little bitch, pouring cold water into my mug. "Jesus," I mutter, dumping the coffee down the sink and starting again with a fresh pod and more sugar.

"Agent McRae?" a voice calls from the doorway to the kitchen. It's one of our young recruits, Veronica, fresh from Quantico.

"Yeah," I reply, only half-listening, the majority of my attention still focused on getting the fucking coffee machine to work.

"You've got a package."

A package? I stir my coffee absent-mindedly. Who's sending packages at three a.m. on a Monday morning?

Not people who are sending anything I want, as a general rule. Packages with nice things tend to be delivered in daylight hours, by men in UPS uniforms, with those little machines you need to sign your name on with a plastic stylus.

Packages outside of normal business hours tend to contain things like severed heads, or bombs, or elaborate envelopes stuffed with glitter from your asshole co-workers.

I abandon the coffee, frowning as I close the space between myself and Veronica in three strides. I take the package from her outstretched hand, touching only the corner with my fingernails as I take it to my desk. "Thank you, Veronica," I call over my shoulder, trying not to draw attention to how odd I must look. I clear everything from my desk with my free hand, setting the package down as gently as I can — in case, you know, *bomb* — and call Isobel over.

She knows straight away by the tone of my voice that something is up, and is standing beside my desk as I read the return sender on the package. There's no return address, just a name.

Avery Capulet.

Isobel looks at me. "Should we open it?"

I step back from my desk ever-so-slightly. "We should wait until it's been inspected."

Isobel scoffs. "Oh, come on," she says. "Bring it down to the lab. If it explodes, at least I won't have to go on a second date with the douchebag from tonight."

I nod in agreement. "And I won't have to watch Frozen again."

We take the package down to the lab, and get one of the crime scene techs to check it over for us. When it seems pretty apparent that the package isn't going to blow our building apart, he opens it with sterile gloves, gently tipping the contents out onto a stainless steel exam table that probably had body parts on it earlier in the day.

Isobel and I, wearing full masks and biohazard scrubs, lay out the items as efficiently as possible. This is going to be the ransom demand, surely.

Sunday's copy of the New York Times is folded up inside the legal-sized envelope, drenched in what looks like blood. Gently, with tweezers, Isobel unfolds the newspaper, and I can't say I'm not surprised with what greets us inside the layers of blood-soaked newsprint.

The engagement ring Avery was wearing. The one worth millions of dollars. Also covered in what appears to be blood. And curled into the middle of the ring, where her finger would have been just hours ago, is a small piece of plastic-coated paper that looks like it's straight from a fortune cookie. Isobel carefully fishes it out of the ring, using two pairs of tweezers to unfurl it.

Isobel and I look at each other at the same time. It's a simple message, but it's not the one I thought it would be. Not a demand for money, or a private jet. Not even a taunting message. Nope, it's almost kind of boring.

Check your email.

So we do, pulling off our gloves and grabbing our cellphones at the same time. And what do you know, we've both got the same message sitting in the top of our individual inboxes.

It's a hyperlink. I click it without worrying about viruses, or bringing down the mainframe, or installing spyware. We can worry about all of that later. Right now, we need to do whatever it takes to find this girl, and that means moving quickly.

My phone has a brief seizure, the screen lighting up and then seeming to turn off a half dozen times, and then a video appears.

I turn my phone to the side, thankful I've got one of the larger iPhones with the big screen. At first, I have to squint to see what's being displayed on the screen, but once I figure out what it is, there's no unseeing.

"Holy fuck," Isobel says next to me, peering at her own phone. "Are you seeing this?"

A girl, who I have to assume is Avery Capulet, based on her appearance as well as the nature of the package, sits on a chair, not a stitch of clothing on her — only blood. A lot of blood. The room isn't well lit, but there's enough light to tell she's been injured badly. She's deathly pale, and shaking, and blindfolded.

"Looks like she's lost a lot of blood," Isobel says. "How long do you think she's got?"

"Not long," I reply, mentally listing all of the things we need to do next.

All the things that will help us to find this girl and bring her home, while we watch on, unable to do a damn thing.

At the top of my list?

Find out where this damn video is coming from, before this poor girl dies.

CHAPTER ELEVEN

AVERY

*T*he thing that wakes me up isn't the throbbing pain in my leg — although that pierces my consciousness soon after rousing. It's my bladder, screaming to be emptied.

Where am I? Am I in the hotel room? Has Will come back?

The knowledge of my situation smashes into me like a freight train running me over as I lie on the tracks, immobile, my limbs sliced to pieces by sharp wheels.

Damn.

It all floods my mind like a tsunami crashing into shore.

The party.

My father being shot, smacking into the pool's

surface before plunging down into it's depths, bleeding and unconscious.

Joshua, practically forcing me down to the loading bay.

The security guards, dropping like flies.

And the two men, the ones wearing the balaclavas, grabbing me, injecting me with something, whatever it was smothering me into a dreamless void.

And after.

Waking up tied to the chair.

The fucking guy, the psychopath, the way he cut off my clothes, made me bleed. A choked sob escapes my lips when I recall his lips kissing between my legs, the low laugh that came from him and vibrated all through my body when he saw how distressed I was at such unwanted intimacy; and then, somehow, I was alone and bleeding.

I don't know what happened after that. I was cold; my thoughts were slow and jumbled. I could feel my heart slowing down, a *thud, thud, thuuuuuud*, like it was trying as hard as it could to find the blood volume to pump something around my battered body.

I can still feel cold air on my thighs, and that makes me panic. *Did he rape me?* I don't feel sore down there. No sorer than I did after Will and I got hot and heavy at the cemetery earlier, anyway. I flex my left hand, missing an engagement ring, but mercifully lacking any ropes or restraints, too. They can have the damn ring. I just want the use of my arms and legs, *thank you very much.* I move my hand between my legs instinctively, cupping myself protectively, but also checking if there is any evidence that they did something to me while I was passed out.

I mean, I'm not in the chair anymore, am I? I'm on my back. It feels soft underneath me. Scratchy, like cheap foam. A mattress. I'm on a mattress. But this ain't a Tempur-Pedic pillow top, no. This is a torture-chamber special. It's damp under me, either with blood, or my pee, or both.

I can't see anything much, but I'm not blindfolded anymore. *Am I still naked?* I use my right hand to touch my chest. I'm wearing something cotton, soft, something that smells faintly of cigarette smoke and men's aftershave, a sandalwood scent that I swear I've smelled before.

A t-shirt. That's what I'm wearing. But it's big. The sleeves are wide, and go down past my elbows. The hem reaches halfway to my knees. And the collar sits loosely around my collarbones. I'm wearing a man's shirt, and underneath it, I'm as naked as the day I was born — and probably as bloody.

I explore my body further, still too weak to try to

sit up. I'm pissed that I've lost so much blood. It sure would have come in handy to be at full strength to try and fight my way out of this place, away from these psychos. My thigh wound is wrapped now, in what feels like gauze or bandages, and there's a little butterfly clip holding the material in place just above my knee. It seems as though someone has cleaned me up.

But I'm still in a dark room, wearing a stranger's shirt, trying to ascertain whether any foreign objects have entered my vagina while I was passed out.

Out of nowhere, a lamp snaps on, and I have to choke back a scream. I sit bolt upright, my head swimming, dangerously close to passing out. Breathless, I drag myself away from the source of light and the hand still gripping it, until a wall stops me, and then I drag myself along that wall until that one stops, too, and I'm wedged in a corner with nowhere to go.

"Don't worry, I didn't fuck you," a low voice says, coming from the same spot where the little light is still shining. It's blue, in the shape of a cloud, a child's nightlight. It casts an eerie blue glow around the room, making me feel even colder than I already am, my teeth chattering uncontrollably. And it illuminates the outline of a man, sitting on the floor in front of me, his knees drawn up to his chest as he watches me.

He's not wearing a balaclava anymore. Is it the same guy? Something about him screams danger, but he sounds … familiar. Like we've met before.

I'm still cupping a hand between my legs, I realize. That's why he said that. *Don't worry, I didn't fuck you*. His tone sounded almost … offended. Like he was upset that I'd think him capable of having sex with his unconscious captive.

I leave my hand where it is, a protective shroud. He put his *mouth* on me. He kissed me there, like a lover would kiss on the mouth. Will's gone down on me more times than I can remember, but he's never, ever kissed me there like *that*. I don't want anyone else kissing me there *ever again*.

Run, my body screams, my mind joining the chorus. *Run!* My limbs are loose and bloodless, my head lolling to one side. I couldn't run even if there were somewhere to go. The shirt covering my body has ridden up at the back while I was moving, and my buttocks are frozen numb on the rough concrete I'm sitting on.

My eyes begin to focus as I continue to pant heavily. I can see the outline of broad shoulders, the faint blacks and reds of tattoos covering his bare chest.

He gets up on his knees and moves closer to me. I shrink into the corner, making myself as small as I can.

"Doesn't mean somebody else didn't sample the goods before I got here," he adds. I shudder, thinking of that, of being thrown onto a mattress and fucked and being totally oblivious to the whole thing.

Every time he speaks, my head pounds relentlessly. Just the sound of his voice is like walking on broken glass. *I know you. Goddamn it, how do I know you?* A fresh wave of nausea rolls through me, and it takes every ounce of my strength to hold down the bile that waits excitedly in my stomach, ready to shoot up and projectile from my mouth.

I start to cry when he stands up, looming in front of me, unbuttoning his jeans. Oh, Jesus. This is it. He's put me on the mattress so he can rape me. He unbuttons his jeans and pushes them down his thighs, revealing muscled legs, covered in tattoos, and a pair of tight black boxer shorts covering the things I want him to keep covered.

"Please, don't," I whimper. "I'll do anything you want. But not that. Please?"

More words tumble out of my mouth that I don't even know I'm saying. Pleading, begging.

Please.

Don't.

It's as if someone has poured cold water on me when his jeans hit me in the face, then land on the mattress in front of me.

"You're freezing," he says, through gritted teeth. "I'm not going to rape you. This is probably hard for a *Capulet* girl to understand, but I don't need to *force* girls to get my dick wet."

I look down at the pair of jeans in shock, then up at him as he moves away from me again. My eyes, once blindfolded, are continuing to adjust to the dim light of the room. "Thank you," I say, taking the jeans and carefully sliding them onto my shaking legs. Why am I *thanking* this guy? Maybe I just want to appease him, behave, avoid aggravating him. But also, I want the jeans on, an added layer of protection for my poor body, something to cover myself with since my panties are long gone, along with the rest of my clothes.

The jeans are too big. They swim on me, but I'm still so grateful for them I could cry. Actually, I could cry regardless. My thigh is starting to hum with pain, and the drugs I was injected with earlier are fucking with my sense of balance something wicked. My lip feels puffy and tastes metallic from where he hit me earlier. And between my thighs, I'm on fire, that unwelcome kiss seared into my flesh and leaving a burn in its wake.

"So," he says. "*Avery Capulet.*" He says my name like the words are poison he's spitting on the ground. "You want to tell me what the fuck is going on?"

That gravelly voice. The mussed-up hair, long on top, short on the sides. He has more tattoos than he did the last time I saw him. The same morning I found my sister dead, floating in our swimming pool, her hair strewn out around her like some kind of mermaid. He was the one who helped me fish her out of the water. He was the one who started CPR, while I lost my fucking mind and screamed for her to wake up. I remember staring at the dragons and the skulls inked onto his arms as he pumped her lifeless chest up and down. They're everywhere, starting under his ears, threading down his neck, right down to the tips of his toes. There's not one part of him that I can see that isn't inked, other than his face.

His bloody, swollen face. He looks like he's been in a fight. Maybe there was a struggle after I passed out.

And finally, I can see his eyes. It's too dim to make out the color, but I can see their shape. I can make out the outline of his lips.

I know who you are.

It's as if somebody has ripped my heart out and smashed it on the dirty floor. I'd know those lips anywhere. They were the first lips I ever kissed.

How could he, of all people, do this?

"You," I whisper, recognizing my captor.

"Hey, Princess," Rome Montague says, his cheery tone dripping with sarcasm. "Or, wait, I guess you're the Queen now, right? It's been forever. When's the last time we hung out, anyway?"

I grit my teeth, wincing as pain throbs in my thigh. I wish I had enough energy to jump up and rip his smug fucking face off. "The last time we *hung out* you were giving my dead sister mouth-to-mouth. But I'm sure you remember that."

His smugness vanishes. His eyes narrow, his breathing quickens — did I just rattle Rome Montague with a single sentence? "How could I forget?" he shoots back, his words full of acid and barbs. "But you're forgetting, aren't you? That's not the last time we saw each other at all."

His words are designed to hurt me, and they work. I hang my head in shame, guilt thick in my throat as I think of what happened to him because of me. "Is this payback, then?"

"Little girl, this wouldn't even be *close* to payback for what you and your family did to me."

Little girl. I might be twenty-five and all grown up, but under Rome's eyes, I'm still a child that needs saving. Only, this time, he's the one I need saving from, not the one who will pick me up in his strong arms and take me to safety.

Grief is like a flash flood; it crashes into me, unexpected, unwanted. I nod as I digest my situation, the shock too fresh for me to think of a way out. I study my surroundings again, different now with the knowledge of who took me. Fitting, even. Because once upon a time, I betrayed Rome Montague in the worst way imaginable. I took away his freedom. In a single moment, a debt was forged that I knew, deep down, he'd come to collect one day.

I just didn't think it would be today. *Not like this.*

"You were kind when I knew you," I whisper. "You weren't cruel. Not like this."

Rome's lips tug up into a smirk. "If you think me bandaging your wounds and giving you my clothes is cruel, I'd hate to see what your definition of kindness is."

"Kindness would be taking me home," I say. My eyes have adjusted somewhat, and I can make out the color of his eyes. They're bright blue, the exact color of the bottom of the pool where we found my sister, still and floating. His eyes are as cold as that pool, too, but there's something about Rome Montague's stare that makes me dizzy with fever. It's the knowing. It's the guilt. Being complicit in the downfall of somebody you used to love burns hotter than any sickness can touch you.

At least, I think I used to love him.

"Kindness would have been you telling the truth," he replies flatly. "But there's no kindness left in you, is there? Only your daddy's blood, pumping through your veins."

My cheeks burn when he talks like that. Because he's right, just like Will was right. All I'll ever be is a girl with daddy issues. A girl who would lie for her father, steal for him, cheat for him. A girl who has done all three of those things.

"Are you going to kill me?" I ask him point-blank.

Rome laughs. "Jesus, girl. Where would be the fun in that?"

Now I feel cold. Part of me wishes he would kill me, but that would be kinder than what I'm sure he has in store for the girl who ruined him.

Rome licks his lips as he studies me. I think of how pathetic I must look: wild, on the floor, bled out like an animal. If my state brings him joy, though, Rome does an excellent job of not showing it.

"It's been so long, I thought maybe you had forgotten me." He makes the words sound almost casual, but I hear the undercurrent in them; the rage. He does think I forgot about him.

I bury my face in my hands so he can't see the haunted look I know is in my eyes, the one that sparks back to life like a match against flint whenever Rome Montague slips into my thoughts.

"I've tried," I say honestly. "Believe me, I've tried."

"So. The little liar can tell the truth on occasion."

"Rome," I protest, looking up at him.

"Don't *Rome* me," he seethes. "You sent me to prison. For two years. *You.*"

"You almost killed my cousin," I say, but there's no conviction behind my words.

"What an evil man I am," Rome says bitterly. "Perhaps I should have closed the door and walked away when I saw what Ty was doing to you. That little fuck deserved every broken bone I gave him, and more."

I swallow painfully. "I know."

"And yet, he got off, scot-free, and I got locked up."

Neither of us says anything for a moment. I'm so dizzy, I need to take a beat just to catch my breath.

"Is that where you got those scars?" I ask finally. "In prison?"

Rome uncrosses his arms, gesturing to the raised silver and red lines that are almost, but not completely, hidden by his tattoos. "What, these?"

I nod.

"Some."

"And the rest?" I press, not sure if I want to know the answer.

Something dark flashes in Rome's eyes for a second. "There are more dangerous places to be a Montague than inside a prison's walls."

I think about that as my leg starts to throb, the pain more insistent now. The drug that knocked me out has started to wear off, and with it, the opiate cushion that separated me from my own nerve endings. I bite down on the insides of my cheeks as I think of my singular wound, and Rome's countless scars. Did each of those hurt him as much as this one hurts me? How did he bear it? And did he curse my name with every sharp edge that split his flesh?

"I think you're the one lying," I whisper. "You are going to kill me."

"If I was going to kill you, you'd already be dead," he says finally.

In my wildest dreams — or my most terrifying

nightmares — never once did I think that I'd be trapped in hell with *him*.

Never once did I think I'd see him again.

Tears prick at my eyes as I think of his mouth on me. But — there were two of them in the loading bay at the Palatial Hotel. So maybe it wasn't Rome who did that. Maybe it was his accomplice. Shouldn't he have my blood all over him if it was him kissing me like that? I'm so confused, everything heavy and slow.

"What have you done?" I whisper. "What are you going to do?"

He doesn't answer me. Instead, he tosses something at me. I don't catch it — I'm too weak and bloodless for that — but it rolls to a stop at my feet anyway. Water.

"You lost a lot of blood," he says. "You should drink something."

I tear at the bottle's lid greedily, not taking a second to taste it cautiously before I start gulping it down. It's cool and fresh and satisfying and … drugged.

Or maybe it's not. Maybe it's just how weak I am, with my heart struggling to pump its meager supply of blood around my body, to keep me alive.

Either way, I'm slumped on the mattress five

minutes later, panting shallow breaths as I try to stay awake. The room spins around me like one of those circus rides, where you're pinned to the side of a spinning disc, and gravity makes you so heavy you can barely blink. That's how I feel now, looking at the boy who has grown into a man, a man who wants nothing more than to destroy my family.

"What do you want?" I whisper in the almost-dark.

His expression is unreadable.

"Rome!" I insist. "What do you *want*?"

"You have no idea what's happening, do you?" he asks, and I can't tell if he's amused, or pained, or both.

My lips feel puffy and numb, my eyelids unbearably heavy. *Why did you bring me here?* I want to ask him, but before I can move my mouth again, everything goes dark.

CHAPTER TWELVE

ROME

I've never claimed to be a good man. In fact, if I had to tell you what kind of person I am, I'd say I'm the very worst. I've done plenty of things that I'd rather forget. Things that I can avoid thinking about until that moment when I close my eyes at night and it all comes flooding back, an avalanche of blood and screams. There's a reason I live alone, in a ruined house that I once tried to burn down. There's a reason people don't want to get close to me. There's a reason I'd rather stay awake for three days straight and screw a girl I don't even like, instead of sleeping.

I'm bad. Bad news. Bad blood. Whatever you want to call it, however you want to spin it: I'm a disease that nobody wants to catch.

But when I see the girl in the ridiculous dress, Avery Capulet, begging for her life in the loading dock of the Palatial Hotel, just as some asshole lowers a black bag over her head and shoves a syringe into her forearm, something forgotten sparks to life.

I came here to confront her cousin, to maybe even kill him. But any thought of Ty Capulet eviscerated as soon as I laid eyes on Avery, looking small in a sea of gun-toting bodyguards and her fiancé, as every single one of them dropped to the ground, leaving only her standing and trapped.

I think I loved her once, even though I hate her now. Even though she damn well ruined my fucking life with her lies. Yeah, even in spite of all that, some protective thing claws at the inside of my chest when I see her being manhandled.

I want to help her. I want to save her.

And I hate myself for that.

"Hey!" I yell, rushing toward Avery as she topples to the ground. I forget about what I'm supposed to be doing here — finding that little fucker, Ty Capulet, and smashing him into a pile of broken bones and blood for trying to get his greasy hands on my formula.

Maybe it's my karma, then, that one of them jumps me and smashes the butt of his gun into my face. I step back, stunned by the blow, reaching for the gun tucked into my waistband. I'm normally so careful, normally the one waiting in the shadows with my gun at the ready, but the sudden sight of the girl being tossed between them like a fucking rag doll caught me off guard. My face explodes in a mess of blood, a crunch of cartilage in my nose telling me something is definitely broken, and the hot, paralyzing crack of a taser in the middle of my chest that takes me down. A fist slams into my face over and over, steel-capped boots in my ribs so hard I feel them crack, and I end up on all fours, crawling away from the boots, dragging myself toward the girl in the dress, who is still lying motionless on the dirty ground, her head completely covered by the black bag. I lift my arm to touch the bag, intending to pull it away from her face, but before I can grip the material a hand grabs the back of my shirt and yanks me away. I switch my attention to the twin fucking ninjas who seem intent on beating me to death so I can stop interrupting their kidnapping mission, and it strikes me as odd that they don't shoot me, too. I mean, I just stood and watched as they shot six guys who looked like private security guards in a matter of seconds, all big, brawny guys armed to the fucking teeth.

One of them tasers me again. The pain is white-hot, but more than that, it stops me from moving. It effectively freezes me in one spot long enough for the dude to grab my head between his gloved palms, lift my head up, and smash my skull back into the asphalt until everything turned a dirty black.

CHAPTER THIRTEEN

ROME

*R*olling on hard ground, and then falling off the edge of something. In that order.

Falling down. Into hell?

I land with a crash, and it's the crash that properly wakes me from my drugged stupor.

Fuck.

I taste blood in my mouth. I'm on something spongy — a mattress? A mattress that's helped to break my fall. But where did I fall from? And where the *fuck* am I?

I can't see. Right. There's a bag over my head. I pull at the material, shaking my head free of its restrictions as I try to decipher my surroundings.

Oh, shit.

This isn't good.

Not at all.

I'm in a room with no outside light. There's a mirror that runs along one side of the room. I swallow as I realize what it is.

That's one-way glass, not a mirror.

I've spent my fair share of time in interrogation rooms over the years, and that's not a fucking mirror. I can only see the dull reflection of the room I'm in, but I have no doubt that whoever is on the other side of that glass can see in here perfectly well.

I look around, searching for an exit. There are two doors in this small room. One looks like it's made of steel, and is set into the wall.

The second door is slightly ajar, and leads to a small bathroom. Also windowless. A place designed for one thing: to keep me from getting out.

Well, to keep *us* from getting out, I think, as I stand up and realize I'm not alone.

"Well, well," I mutter, clenching my teeth so hard they might crack in my mouth. "What do we have here?"

A beautiful woman, completely naked, and tied to a chair, legs spread and wearing a pair of patent leather fuck-me-now stilettos. Normally I'd call that an open invitation, but something about the way she's teetering on the edge of death stops me from trying my best pick-up lines on her. I like to be in charge in the bedroom, but I prefer my girls to fight back. This one looks like I'd be risking necrophilia if I got too carried away.

I open my mouth, addressing nobody in particular. "If you're trying to Punk me, Ashton Kutcher, this is a little much."

I stare at the girl in front of me. She's covered in blood, a nasty wound running along the inside of one thigh that seeps blood onto the chair. The same blood rushes to the edge of the seat and plinks down onto the floor in time with my thundering pulse, drip, drip, drip.

I reach instinctively for the gun I always shove into the back of my jeans. Gone. The stash of my drug is gone from my left pocket. Motherfuckers. The switchblade from my right pocket is gone too, leaving me with nothing but the clothes I'm wearing, the red heart-shaped pills Rosaline tried to steal stashed deep in my pocket, and a girl whose identity is rapidly becoming apparent to me as I study her face with my adjusting eyes. Everything from the Palatial Hotel comes rushing back, even as I try to convince myself this isn't happening.

Fuck. It can't be her.

It *is* her.

Avery.

Avery Capulet.

The urge to rush to her side and get her out of these binds bubbles up inside me, frenetic and anxious. But my desire to help her is quickly tamped down by my memory of everything that's transpired since the last time I saw her. In the years since our families went from loyal allies to bitter enemies, our meetings, fleeting as they were, always happened under the cover of secrecy. A hall pass in study period to meet in locker rooms and bathroom stalls. A shared cigarette behind the stables where her beloved horses were kept. A stolen glance between a sophomore (her) and a senior (me) in the hallways of Verona's most exclusive preparatory college. We were supposed to hate each other back then, but I could never bring myself to fall in line with the hate I held for the rest of her family. I knew she was her father's pawn. I still burned for her anyway.

---

*A*nd after her sister died, I only saw her one more time — the day she got on the stand in court and perjured her little Capulet heart out. The day her lies sent me to prison. The day she destroyed whatever feverish teenage love I thought I'd had for her, and replaced it with a cold, brutal hatred.

That was almost ten years ago, and the most I've ever seen her since then is in momentary flashes through the window of my ruined mansion, as she parked her car or dove into her pool — at least, until they put up the privacy hedges and destroyed my view. After that, the best chance I had of catching a look at her was on gossip sites and in the newspapers. It didn't matter, though. I still remembered how the little hollow of her collarbone tasted, how her hair felt in my fist. A fucking *privacy hedge* wasn't going to take those things from me.

Now somebody — who, I can't even begin to figure out — has served her up to me like Thanksgiving dinner with all the trimmings, the kind so delicious you'd glut yourself to the point of sickness just to devour it. I've never been that interested in food, but I'd gorge myself on a girl like Avery Capulet until there was nothing of her left, and still want more.

Even with the blood.

Maybe *especially* with the blood.

I push away the lust in my belly, seeing her laid out like this. Because really, she does look like she's about to bleed to death. I'm groggy from the drugs, my head pounding from being kicked while I was down, but I've still got my bearings enough to know that if she dies, I'm going to look like the bad guy.

A set up. Is somebody setting me up?

Who?

I begin to mentally catalog my mortal enemies, until I realize there are too many and I'm not yet privy to whatever this game is. I can't make a move until I've been dealt all the cards, so I do what my conscience has been screaming at me to do: I help the damn girl.

Right now I know nothing. Can presume nothing. Just because we're enemies, doesn't mean she has anything to do with this. We also share other, mutual enemies. Some of the other influential families in this city dislike both of our families. Then there are the Russians. Cameras and serial killings are probably too sophisticated for them, but what the fuck do I know? There are rival drug cartels who don't like the way her father launders blood money from certain associates through his banks and refuses to touch funds from others. All of these enemies don't even cover the legitimate business dealings her father has that could have gone awry and triggered a revenge plot against the family.

Let he who is without sin cast the first stone, my father would say to me. I've been a sinner all my life.

So I do what I can for her; I make sure for now, that Avery Capulet doesn't die.

I untie her from the chair, wincing as she slumps in my arms, naked and bloody and deep in some unconscious world I'm not privy to. I realize as I lay her on the thin mattress that I haven't touched this girl in almost a decade. She still uses the same *fucking* shampoo. I lean in a little without realizing, breathing in the fresh smell of oranges that clings to her dark hair, and then I set to making sure she doesn't bleed to death in front of me.

I bandage her wound with dressings I find in a medical kit in the bathroom. The kit is small, but stocked with all manner of things — gauze, rubbing alcohol, superglue. *Scissors*. My eyes light up when I see those. I slide them under the mattress as casually as possible, trying to ascertain which of the seven goddamn cameras I can block with my body. Whoever is watching us probably saw me. Whatever. As if they'd expect me to give up without a fight.

I have to superglue Avery's thigh wound shut to stop the bleeding. I have no idea if I've made things worse, if she'll somehow keep bleeding subcutaneously, if superglue is going to slowly poison her. She's shaking, shivering, her whole body covered in gooseflesh. Her nipples look hard enough to cut through the glass window that separates us from freedom, even though I try really, really hard not to look at them. I take off my t-shirt and dress her in it, covering her as best I can, wincing every time I accidentally touch one of the fresh bruises that continue to spring up on her pale skin like some macabre watercolor painting.

The whole time, she stays limp, her pulse slow and thready. I try to pretend I don't care. That it wouldn't destroy any semblance of a life I have left if she died from this. But I guess I'm a liar, too. Because deep down, I know if anything happened to her, if she died, I'd most likely lay down on this dirty floor, swallow the pills I still have in my pocket, and die right beside her.

I sit in the corner and watch her breathe. It's so dark in here, I can't make out any detail of anything. Just the steady rise and fall of her chest, the proof that, moment to moment, she's still alive.

Then, after what seems like forever, Avery Capulet wakes up.

Fear in her eyes as she shrinks away from me. That fills me with a grief I've never known. Does she really think I could ever hurt her like this?

She does, I can tell, at least at first.

Because eventually, the real madman in all of this

comes back into the room, a gun in his hand, a mask covering his face.

And that's when the nightmare really begins.

His gun holds me at bay at first. As he picks Avery up and throws her down on the table that sits in the middle of the room. She's still wearing my shirt, but she's got my jeans on, too. I'm the half-naked idiot in the corner, my palms raised in false surrender as I watch him put a revolver in her fucking mouth and push it so far, she gags.

A gun? You're putting a fucking gun in her mouth?

He cocks the hammer and I crouch down, reaching for the scissors tucked safely under the mattress.

The next part happens in slow motion. I yell something at him — I'm not sure what, now. Get away from her, or Don't fucking touch her, or something like that. Whatever it is, I've got the scissors in my hand, and I'm moving toward him, every muscle in my body coiled and ready to attack. I have momentum. I have speed. I have a weapon in my hand.

And then the world explodes.

Not the whole world, you understand? Just mine. The gun isn't in Avery's mouth anymore. It's pointed at me, and I'm slammed against the wall by the force of a bullet.

I bite down on my tongue when the bullet enters my flesh. I taste blood in my mouth as I bleed rivers from a dirty hole in my bare shoulder. I crumple like a rag doll, choking on the pain as my thoughts pulse in time with my heart.

I've been shot. I've been shot. I've been shot.

It's bad for me. I might die. But it's worse for her. There is a violence in tenderness, and whoever this man is, he shows it to her. I want to move. I want to save her. But all I can do is watch.

I've been shot. I've been shot. *I've been shot.*

CHAPTER FOURTEEN

AVERY

I'm woken by rough hands, picking me up and dragging me to my feet. In the split-second that I first come to, I forget what's happened. Confusion floods me as I question everything — where I am, what's happening, who's grabbing me. Instinctively, I strike out with my closed fist, looking to hit whoever has hold of me.

Why can't I see anything?

My fist hits what feels like a hard cheekbone covered in cloth, and the person holding on to me grunts in pain. That's satisfying. But my satisfaction is short-lived, as a fist returns the blow out of nowhere, hitting me square in the nose. I gasp as blood explodes from my nostrils, the pain white-hot and unexpected, and for a moment I can't hear anything but a static buzz.

"Hey!" I hear a male voice protest. Rome. It's *Rome.* My ears are still ringing, and his voice sounds faraway. Like I'm underwater. Like I'm drowning. Can't see. Can't see. It's like one of the nightmares I have almost every night. Nightmares where it's me drowning instead of Adeline, and it's Rome Montague's hand fisted in my hair, holding me under until I take a breath and fill my lungs with cold water.

"Leave her alone!" Rome roars.

That's odd.

Isn't Rome meant to be the one punching me? Not the one defending me? Wouldn't my pain please him?

I don't have long to think about that before I feel hands at my throat, dragging me.

"Don't touch her. Don't *fucking* touch her!"

Gloved fingers squeeze at my cheeks, forcing my mouth open. I try to bite down, to close my mouth, but whoever this guy is — he's too strong, and I'm too drugged to react quickly enough. Something cold and metallic is shoved between my teeth. I don't register what it is at first — until I hear the click.

"A gun!?" Rome yells, at the same time I realize, yes, there's a gun in my mouth. A revolver. The clicking sound was the hammer being cocked.

I have a loaded gun in my mouth. I whimper around the cold gun barrel as it scrapes against my teeth, trying not to gag.

Why can't I see? Am I blind?

"You're putting a gun in her mouth?" Rome's voice echoes through the tiny room.

I'm trying desperately to breathe evenly. I've never considered what a gun barrel might taste like before, but even if I had, I could not have imagined *this*. The metal is cold, and it makes a sickening scrape against my teeth as my captor forces it past my lips. It tastes oily, and metallic, and I'm struck for the first time by how similar a gun tastes to blood.

"Jesus, fuck, leave her alone," Rome grinds out. I can hear the raw edge of panic in his voice, a voice that was controlled before.

Not anymore. Not down here. We're in the wild, now. The gun is suddenly gone from my mouth, and I suck in deep breaths, choking on the air I didn't realize I needed.

A hand comes to rest at the base of my throat again. I blink rapidly, *why can't I see?* I try so hard to grab onto my consciousness long enough to figure out what's happening.

There's material against my eyelashes. I'm blindfolded again, still rubbery and pliant from the drugs.

That's why I can't see. I want to fight back, to kick and claw at the violent hands at my throat, but it's such an effort to even breathe. All of my energy was focused on that single punch, and now I'm ready to pass out again.

My prayers are answered; the hands let go of me. I fall through the air for a split-second, and then I'm landing on something hard, something flat that the back of my head thwacks against. It's blissful, that millisecond when I'm suspended mid-air, a relieved moan escaping my lips as I fall in slow-motion. My captor's hands are no longer on me. But the hard surface of what feels like a table breaks my fall, knocking the wind out of me. I'm sprawled awkwardly, my legs bent at the knee, dangling off the edge of what must be a table, or a countertop. With every ounce of energy I possess, I lift my arms to my face and tear off the material blindfolding me.

A hand immediately goes around my throat again, as I take in the features — or rather, the lack of features — of the man cutting off my air supply. He's dressed differently now, a black hoodie pulled snug around his ears, the black balaclava still on under-neath. The hoodie casts a shadow over his face, and I can't make out any of his features; not the color of his eyes, the only things visible through the twin holes in the tight material, nor the shape of his head. *Nothing.* I follow his outstretched arm, the one that isn't pinning my throat, finding the gun in his hand. It's pointed at the corner where Rome's voice was coming from.

A hand grabs at my wrists, yanking them above my head, and a second later I feel heavy metal circling them. I try to move my arms, but they're stuck — handcuffed to the top of the table. It's so dark in here, I can barely make out anything other than superficial outlines.

I turn my head to the side, my eyes struggling to make out the figure in the corner.

"Fuck her," a deep, distorted voice sounds from the hoodie guy. He's looking at the figure in the corner.

He's looking at Rome.

My captor's voice is unnaturally deep, as if there's something against his mouth, under that black mask, that's changing the sound. He sounds like a mixture of Christian Bale's gravel Batman voice, and the abrasive voice-changer the murderers used in the Scream movies. It probably wouldn't be so terrifying if I were listening to it on a TV screen, but I'm not, am I? This is real life. This is happening. This isn't make-believe, or a nightmare I can wake up from.

This is brutal, violent truth, and it's only about to get worse.

"Fuck her, or I will," the deep voice repeats.

A wail starts deep in my belly and fills the room. *Fuck her*. Of course I'm chained to a table with no way to escape. Of course there's blood all over my face, down my throat, making me cough every time it drips a little down my nasal passages and slides back down my throat. Of course I'm wearing the clothes Rome gave me while he stands in the corner wearing nothing but his boxer shorts. *Of course.*

Rome moves closer to the table. "I'm not *fucking* her," he spits. "And you're not touching her."

In the next moment, three things happen that make me understand that things are not the way I believed them to be. Firstly, Rome charges at the hoodie guy. Second, there is a deafening shot as hoodie guy pulls out a gun and shoots Rome, who goes flying back into the wall with a crash, sliding down to the floor and leaving an oily streak of red in his wake.

Nonononono.

My ears scream at the sudden gunshot, their timbre settling to a steady ringing that makes my teeth hum and drowns everything else out to static buzz. My jeans — Rome's jeans — are ripped away from me, and I'm naked from the waist down again. Masked Psycho doesn't bother getting the t-shirt off this time, I guess because my hands are restrained above my head. Instead, he pushes the shirt up my stomach, right up to my neck, so that my tits are visible. He presses a hand over my mouth to stop the screams that I can't control, and if I thought his mouth on me was bad, this is something unthinkable. The faceless nightmare of a man who looms over me undoes his fly slowly, every movement a taunt of what's to come, as we communicate silently. He cocks his head to the side and eases the pressure of his palm on my face just slightly, and somehow I know what he means. He'll take the hand away if I stop screaming.

I nod, pressing my lips together as tightly as possible, and the hand on my mouth disappears. I take a great gulp of air.

"You shot him," I say, dazed.

My captor nods. My ears scream with static. Fingers drag up my thigh, closing in on their destination with horrifying speed.

"Please don't," I beg, craning my neck. "I'll do anything."

A low chuckle sounds from under his mask, the vibration traveling through his fingers that clutch my thigh, sweeping through my body, a horror I don't fully understand but know I will. His fingers leave my thigh and sweep across my pussy, my muscles tensing in shock. "Anything?"

I let my head loll back onto the table, the weight of holding my head up too painful. "Anything but *that*."

His leather-gloved fingers reach around my neck and squeeze, as he uses his other hand to reach for something in his pocket.

My entire body starts to shake violently, and he's barely touched me. My worst nightmare is to be raped. I don't accept drinks from strangers, I never walk alone at night, and there's been exactly one man in my bed the past eight years - Will, the guy I've been madly in love with. The kind of guy who wouldn't so much as ask me twice if I said I didn't want to have sex. Because my nightmare isn't just rooted in the fact that I'm a woman, from a powerful family, a family with more enemies than we could ever count. My worst fear is so precise because *it's happened before*.

I foolishly thought the money and the Capulet name and the bodyguards and my general sense of extreme caution in life would mean that I'd always be safe, from that day forth. Something bad happened to me when I was younger because I had been careless. Foolish. Rebellious. A secret party, a single cup of something sweet, laced without my knowledge, and I'd been a sitting duck. An easy fuck. A girl who blacked out. A girl who woke up in a dark room with no underwear and blood where I had been broken without my consent. I blamed myself, because if I had been at home, in bed, asleep, like I was supposed to be, it would never have happened.

At least, that's what my uncle Enzo said when he found out what had happened to me.

I believed him.

I changed everything to make sure I would always be safe, so that nobody could ever hurt me like that again. And in my arrogance, I felt completely secure.

How wrong I was.

Look at where I am.

My captor's large body leans over mine, blocking out much of the weak light. He takes one of his leather gloves off, trailing his fingers along my slit before circling my clit gently. Gently - like a lover would. I thrash around, trying to escape his touch, but all I succeed in doing is making the friction of his finger against me more intense. I stop moving, tensing my fists, my abdominal muscles, my ass, everything.

"*Please stop*," I whisper, staring up at the ceiling, feeling hot tears roll from the corners of my eyes and trace their way down my temples, slowly bleeding into my hairline. God, I hate to beg. It fills me with rage. I've never begged for anything in my life, except perhaps this morning, when I begged my father to not have to marry Joshua Grayson.

A sob rocks my chest, piercing the statue stillness I've forced my body to become, my lungs gasping for breath as everything narrows. *A panic attack.* What fucking use is a panic attack going to do for me right now?

Though, maybe I'll pass out if I hyperventilate enough. It's happened before. My blackouts have been few and far between, but dramatic enough when they come in the middle of a funeral, or a party, or in a hospital corridor when you discover your sister is, indeed, dead. Here? If I pass out, this asshole will probably set me on fire to wake me up again.

Still, that's the thing about a panic attack. It creeps up and *attacks* you. It's happening. It's not like I have a choice in the matter. Breathing exercises might work in social situations, and meditation apps might work when you're at a yoga retreat in Cabo, but when your captor is finger-fucking you in the dark after shooting your fellow captive, a panic attack goes and goes without any possible intervention.

I sob and gasp for air as his finger moves almost casually against my clit.

If he does this to me, I want it to hurt. It makes it easier if it hurts. I don't want his gentle touch. I don't want his steady rub.

And I think he knows that.

Jesus fucking Christ, who is this guy? How the fuck does he know that the only thing more terrifying than him brutally raping me is him gently bringing me to orgasm as if I want it?

He stops momentarily, and it takes every ounce of self-control that I possess to stop from raising my hips to find his finger again. Shame floods through my body, a poison that spreads to every extremity, and I imagine my naked body blazing red with embarrassment. *Just make it cold*, I wish feverishly. *Make it clinical. Make it terrible, if you're going to steal this from me. Don't make it feel like the most pleasurable feeling I've had since I fucked Will in the mausoleum.*

But I can't say that. I can't spoon feed this psychopath with all of the things that frighten me the most. He'll take each one, mold them into shiny daggers, and use them to make me bleed.

The crinkle of a condom wrapper has me shaking

even more violently. *This is happening. It's fucking happening.* I crane my head up and to the side, needing to know what he's doing, desperate to find a way to stop him. In my peripheral vision, I see Rome, his chest rising and falling too quickly, one hand staunching the river of blood pumping from his shoulder. He's so close I could almost reach out and touch him, but my hands are shackled, and what could I do, anyway? I focus my attention on my captor — our captor — wincing as I see him rolling a condom onto his erection, the tip of his cock dark with arousal. A tiny part of me is relieved he's wearing protection, because I don't want any part of him left inside me after this horror is finally over. But on the other hand, a condom means no DNA, and if I survive this, am I really going to live the rest of my life looking over my shoulder, wondering when he's going to show up and grab me again?

Is that how this ends? Without an ending at all?

Then I remember the XO he painted on my chest in my own blood and all thoughts of survival float away with the rest of my hope. The XO killer doesn't leave survivors.

He leaves bodies.

He must notice me eyeing his condom-wrapped dick intently. He pushes my thighs apart so hard I feel like I might snap in two, making room for his body between my spread legs as I fight to press them closed. The mask muffles his sigh, as he pushes the tip of his cock against my entrance and stays there.

Resignation punches me in the gut as the fight goes out of me. My knees fall open, no force required to keep them apart anymore. He's inside me, now, even though he hasn't seated himself fully inside me. He's breached my body, and I'm too weak to keep struggling. The back of my head hits the table with a resounding thud, and I turn it to the side, exhausted.

Rome. I blink the film of tears away from my eyes, trying to focus on him through the haze of salt water flooding my vision. He's in a bad way — worse than me — and I feel my heartbeat speed up when I see how ashen his skin is. Even in this weak light, it's impossible to miss the grey pallor he's suddenly taken on, the blood everywhere, the glassy film over his eyes as he meets my eyes, but doesn't entirely see me.

At least, I don't think he sees me. His stare is too fixed, his expression too distant. For a moment, I wonder if he's dead. But then he mouths *I'm sorry* to me, and my heart fucking shatters.

Our captor starts circling my clit again, long, deliberate strokes with his thumb that make my body react eagerly, despite my abject horror. I hate this man. I want to sit up and tear his eyes out, choke him to death with my bare hands, slice away at his flesh until he bleeds out at my feet. I've never much had the stomach for blood, but here, in this room, the air thick with the copper scent of Capulet and Montague blood as it all mixes together — I thirst for the spilling of *this* madman's lifeblood like nothing else.

"So wet," he says, pulling away a little so that he can trail the head of his cock through my soaked pussy lips, the lust in his voice evident even underneath whatever it is that's altering his voice inside that mask. I make a mental note to rip his mask off the moment I have my hands free, and at least see who he is before he murders me.

I feel blood rise in my cheeks when he says that, because it's true. I *am* wet, not because I want this, but because he's pressing my flesh in ways that reduce it to the most animalistic of vessels. I am a lioness in the savannah, forced down in the dirt as a larger male lion does whatever he pleases to her, while she growls and lies still and waits for it to be over. We're in the wild, down here, and we're nothing but animals writhing in sweat and blood.

His thumb continues to draw pleasure from my treacherous body, a pleasant throb intensifying deep in my belly that I can't run away from. I bite down on the inside of my cheek, digging my fingernails into my palms at the same time to distract myself with the pain. He's patient, though, and somehow, even though I've never experienced a forced orgasm before, I know instinctively that I'm on the edge of breaking apart underneath his savage touch.

Do I bear down? Do I hold my breath? Do I scream? I frantically catalog my limited options to dull the frenetic sparks building deep inside my womb, as I try desperately to hold back the tsunami of white-hot pleasure I can hear roaring toward me.

"Do it," my captor demands.

"Fuck you!" I spit back.

He slaps me across the face so hard, I can feel my ear buzzing loudly in protest. I'm once again eye-to-eye with Rome, whose eyes are rolling around in his head something vicious. He looks freakishly blood-less, his pale skin almost translucent, but when he catches my eye again he seems to focus in on me. The tattoos covering his body seem even brighter in the absence of the normal tan his skin would have. He looks like a ghost. Soon, he might actually become one. And for some reason, that makes me sadder than I thought possible.

I'm so tired. So, so weary. The slap jolted me out of my focused detachment, and with the fresh pain seared into my cheek I start to float away, still acutely aware of the man nudging my entrance with his swollen cock, his thumb massaging my bundle of nerves to tortured heights I've never experienced before. I lock eyes with Rome, the blue in his a welcome distraction in the near-darkness. In my mind, I am floating in the azure-blue ocean of Rome Montague's eyes as a tsunami of oxytocin slams into me and pulls me under, a choked moan ripped from my mouth as my hips press forward, eager to be filled up. My physical body betrays me entirely, achingly empty as I come so hard, so painfully, I almost black out.

But I don't black out. I keep my eyes trained on Rome Montague as I wait out the pleasure and pain, the tiny lighter-blue flecks in his stormy eyes like flames that I hold on to, little reflections of light in the darkness. Sadness spreads through my chest as my orgasm fades, as I watch Rome struggle to breathe. *Don't you die and leave me here alone*, I think, my fear at losing him sudden and visceral … and strangely out of place. *Don't you fucking die on me, Rome Montague.* I open my mouth to say … I don't know. To say something. His name.

Rome, I mouth, no sound coming out.

"Rome," I choke, my eyes never leaving his,

because I won't even give my captor the satisfaction of my gaze as he destroys me completely.

Rome blinks, and seems to straighten a little. I'm relieved, for one tiny second in time, and then I'm screaming again as, without warning, the man draped over my body slams into me, hard and deep and vicious.

He doesn't keep fucking me, though. My captor pulls out of me as I'm looking at Rome, his cock immediately replaced by his fingers. At first I'm confused, and then I'm filled with dread.

"What is this?" he growls, his featureless face only amplified by whatever is changing his voice under that mask. I open my mouth to protest as he wraps his fingers around one of the strings attached to my IUD and tugs.

I scream. Louder than I've ever screamed in my life. Everything in my vision turns red as a stabbing pain deep inside my womb spreads, sharp and clear and utterly unbearable.

He tugs again. *Oh, God.* He thinks I'm wearing a tampon, I suppose, but I'm not. The strings are attached to the brand-new IUD I had fitted in my doctor's office a few weeks ago, a tiny, plastic T-shaped device that sits in the bottom of my uterus, the attached strings just outside my cervix.

I had it updated to a new one, knowing that my birthday was drawing closer, guessing that my father would have something up his sleeve concerning myself and Joshua and how eager he was to marry me off so I could start bearing Capulet heirs. I chose one of the little plastic devices that releases a measured dose of hormones that prevent pregnancy for five whole years. I was supposed to go back to the doctor the day after my birthday to have the strings attached to the IUD trimmed down, so they wouldn't bother me or anyone I might be sleeping with.

I vaguely recall Will mentioning something about the little strings attached to the device when we had sex the week after I had it inserted. He said he could feel them, but he didn't seem too bothered. This guy, on the other hand — he's pulling so hard it feels like he's going to rip my uterus out with his bare hands. I don't even have my hands free to try to fight his away — I'm completely useless. I try to string words together to warn him.

PleaseIt'sAnIUDPleaseDon'tPullItPleaseDon't-Please

I don't even know what I'm saying. Words are falling out of my mouth unbidden, as the pain in my womb intensifies and I feel what I think is blood coming out of me. I had to read a pamphlet and sign a waiver before the doctor would implant the tiny device, a legal document full of statistics and rare side-effects that include sudden death if the IUD is inserted incorrectly, or perforates the uterus. Which is *exact-fucking-ly* what it feels like is happening right now.

Is this how I die? Am I going to bleed to death thanks to my fucking birth control? The irony isn't completely lost on me, but I'm more concerned with getting this guy to stop pulling on it before he tears my insides apart.

He takes his hands away. "Explain."

The pain recedes somewhat, since he's no longer pulling the damn thing, but it's still sharp enough that the room is spinning around me with wild abandon.

"It's an IUD," I say quickly, the bright edge of pain biting down on me as I try to speak. "It's a birth control implant. It's in my uterus. If you pull it out, I'll probably bleed to death."

Well, maybe I won't — plenty of women pull theirs out with no problems whatsoever — but after the doctor inserting it just a few weeks ago called my cervix the "cutest little cervix he's ever seen," I'm pretty sure I'd be horrifically injured if he kept pulling until the device was out of me.

"Take it out," he orders. I open my mouth to

protest when I realize he's reaching for my hands. Undoing the metal cuffs that hold my arms up. He pulls me to my feet, the rush of blood to my numb arms a shock. My knees buckle immediately, even as I try to stand. *I need to pull his mask off*, I think. *I need to see who he is.*

"Can't," I pant. "I need surgery to take it out."

That makes him angry. I can't see his face, but I can feel how his body tenses. He spins me around, pliable little puppet I am, and forces me down onto the table so that my palms are flat against the wood grains. I try to thrash again, to get away from his grip, but before I can do anything his fingers snake through my hair and grip, pulling at my scalp as he slams the side of my head down onto the table's unforgiving surface. I make one last move to try to buck him off of me, fully aware that he's not finished raping me, not by a long shot — and that damn gun is in his hand again, pressed against my cheekbone.

I go limp. I'd like to say I'm brave enough to risk being shot in the name of fighting to get away, but the reality is, the sight of Rome bleeding to death on the floor has me compliant. The Capulet blood that roars in my head, a steady, aching thump, begs me to resist him, even if it means certain death. The prehistoric part of my brain, however, the fight, fight or freeze programming, jams on freeze. I'm frozen. Another sob falls from my mouth as he pushes back into me, thrust after violent thrust. Maybe it's not as deep for him like this, fucking me from behind, with me draped over the table face-down. Or maybe it hurts him the way it hurts me. Maybe it's worth the pain for him.

He doesn't speak again. He just ruts into me, again and again. *Please let it be over soon.* I keep focused on Rome, his eyes closed now, and I don't think I blink until there's a groan, a final violent thrust as my rapist beds into me, and the pulse of knowing he's finished.

CHAPTER FIFTEEN

ROME

*S*he mouths my fucking name while he's raping her.

Rome...

And she lets out a little breath of air as she moves her mouth. The smell of sex and sweat and blood fills the tiny room we're in, and inside my chest, my heart slows down.

I've been stabbed before. Walked through fire - I have the scars up my arms to prove it, or at least I did until I tattooed over them. But being shot?

Being shot is a first for me.

And I've gotta say, it hurts like a motherfucker. It hurts more than being stabbed, but less than being burnt alive. The pain from standing in the middle of a burning building as flames lick your flesh is a pain that consumes your every nerve ending until your entire body screams. Being stabbed is more dull, especially when it's in the back, and you weren't expecting it. When I was stabbed in prison, I thought I'd been punched at first. The knife was sharp, but the pain was dull. It wasn't until the asshole who stabbed me wrenched his knife out of my side and plunged it back in that I understood what he was doing. The sharp edge of pain wouldn't come until much, much later, in the aftermath, after he'd been wrestled to the ground and I was being stitched up in the infirmary with no painkillers.

But being *shot.* Sweet Mother Mary, being shot is a whole new level of agony. It's like being stabbed with fire, the pain localized as it throbs in tune with my heart. *Thump.Thump.Thump.* I can feel more of my blood leaving my body with every beat of my heart, and that freaks me out. I put my left hand over my right shoulder, feeling the mess of broken flesh underneath my palm, the rush of blood as it finds its way out of my veins and slides down my arm. Between Avery and I, it's like a damn slaughterhouse in here, and the only man left standing is a man whose identity I have no idea of.

CHAPTER SIXTEEN

AVERY

*Y*ou know those moments where you thought you knew what was happening, only to have your whole world crumble as the illusion you believed was reality broke apart and showed the truth?

That moment, for me, is when the bullet hits Rome Montague's shoulder and embeds itself in his body. And the moments after, as I watch him hit the wall behind him and slide to the floor, his eyes wide with shock, his bullet wound spurting blood.

You don't shoot your co-kidnappers.

And that's the moment I realize the man I thought was part of my kidnapping - maybe even the master-mind of it - isn't a part of it at all.

Rome Montague is a hostage, same as me. I didn't

understand at first, because he was unbloodied and untouched and I was — well, very bloodied, very touched — and he was just so fucking arrogant when I woke up.

He gave you his clothes, and you were a bitch to him. Guilt crashes into me like waves crashing into rocks, hard and fast and unrelenting.

He literally gave you everything he had on him, save for his underwear, and you thought he was your enemy.

Well, he's still my enemy, but in this room, in this hell, he might be the only ally I have.

My ally who is bleeding to death before my eyes.

We're alone now. After our captor finished with me, he left, the heavy steel door leading into the room closing with a resounding thunk.

The room is almost dark again, save for the tiny kid's nightlight in the shape of a puffy blue cloud that sits in the corner. It casts an eerie glow across the room, making Rome look like some kind of tattooed vampire. A tattooed vampire covered in blood. I don't think I've ever seen so much blood in my life. His and mine, all mixed together in here, wherever here is.

With difficulty, I crawl down from the table to the floor, fresh blood slick between my thighs as I try to ignore the sharp throb in my belly. I tug Rome's shirt back over myself, the edge grazing the tops of my thighs. I forget the jeans. By the time I find them and put them back on, Rome might be dead.

If he isn't already.

"Rome?" I whisper, crawling to him. He's slumped on the mattress now, his eyes closed. "Fuck," I whisper. Tears bite at my eyes, and I'm too tired to stop them from falling. I pull Rome onto my lap, using my hands to apply pressure over his wound. "Rome!?"

He doesn't rouse. He's still breathing, though, and that spurs me. Instinctively, I know I have to find something to stem the bleeding. If I have bandages on, then there must be some, somewhere. I look around the room, and that's when I notice the cameras for the first time.

"Oh, God," I choke. I want to know who's watching us. I want to kill them. But first, I want to get their attention.

"Hey!" I scream, looking up at the cameras in my sight. "Hey, asshole! He needs a doctor or he's going to die!"

I look back down at Rome, my hair falling over his face like a veil. His eyes are open, now, bloodshot and blue, and he's trying to sit up.

"Oh my God, you're awake." Without thinking, I lean down and kiss him on the lips. It's nothing, really, barely a brush of my lips across his, but some of the color returns to his cheeks. His eyes widen when I do that. I swallow back panicked sobs, nervous laughter bubbling through. "Don't move. You've been shot."

One side of his mouth quirks up, with difficulty. "No shit."

I ignore his sarcasm. If he's still able to mouth off, he's not that close to death. At least, I hope.

"I thought you were dead," I say, still holding one hand over his bullet wound, my other coming to rest on the side of his face.

Rome's eyes roll back in his head. "I will be in about five minutes," he coughs, fresh blood appearing on his lower lip. Shit. I think blood in his mouth means he's got a punctured lung, or something.

"Bullshit," I say, even though we both know he might be. "Rome Montague isn't about to let one little bullet kill him. Montagues are more stubborn than that."

He coughs again, more blood trailing from the side of his mouth. "Are you okay?" he asks with diffi-culty. I fight the urge to roll my eyes. Really? He's literally dying in my arms, and he's asking how I am?

"You should see the other guy," I mutter.

"Avery," Rome says slowly. "I'm sorry. If I can't stay awake. I'm sorry." He's pressing something into my hand with his. I look down to see what it is — a pair of scissors.

"Hide them," he mumbles, taking a ragged breath in that makes his whole body shake. "Stab him. Get yourself out of here."

I grit my teeth, closing my fingers around the scissors. "Don't fucking die on me," I demand, but really, I'm begging. For a girl who's never begged for anything, today sure has been full of it. I hate it, but I'd beg Rome for the rest of my life it meant he wouldn't die right now. We might be enemies, but I loved him once, a very long time ago. And he only got shot because he was trying to protect me from that fucking psychopath who put us here.

"I'm trying really hard not to," Rome mutters. Still a smartass, even with his dying breaths. Well, fuck it. I'm not going to just sit here with him in my lap and watch him slowly fade to nothing. I look up at the cameras, formulating a plan. I ease Rome off me as gently as possible so he's laying on the mattress, getting to my feet. My legs are shaking uncontrollably, and I'm on the verge of passing out, but somehow, the thought of losing Rome and being left in this room by myself gives me the strength to stand.

"Hey, motherfucker!" I yell, my voice hoarse, but still loud. I pull my hair away from my neck with one hand, aiming the pointy end of the scissors at my jugular with the other. "Get him a doctor or I swear to God, I'll kill myself right now!" Would I have the courage to stab myself in the neck? I'm not really sure, but my voice sounds confident enough.

I look down at Rome, whose eyebrows are raised slightly as he watches me silently. It occurs to me, in that moment, that it probably wouldn't be the worst thing for Rome to see me kill myself with a pair of surgical scissors. He blames me for ruining his life, after all. What's a little suicide between mortal enemies? But he doesn't look amused. He's shaking his head. "Don't— " he says to me. I don't get to hear the rest of his sentence, though, because the heavy steel door in the wall bursts open, the man in black brandishing a new gun. I blink, staring at the weapon he's pointing at me. I've seen one of those before. It's not a gun with bullets in it. He pulls the trigger and I feel a sharp sting in my chest. "Ow," I say, staring down at the tranquilizer dart now lodged neatly above my left breast.

It hurts. Everything seems to move in slow

motion. I yank the dart out of my chest and it clatters to the ground, forgotten. The sedative burns as it spreads through my chest, as my already weak knees buckle and I end up kneeling on the mattress beside Rome. The scissors are still clutched in my hand, my arm hanging loosely by my side. It takes a couple of minutes for the sedative to work its magic and send me off to sleep. I crawl around on the mattress, moaning, trying to stay conscious, and then I feel a hand over mine. I look down to see Rome's hand clutching mine. That's the last thing I see before I fall face-first on the thin bedding beside him.

CHAPTER SEVENTEEN

ROME

*F*or someone who shot me, the motherfucker wearing a mask sure does go to a great deal of effort to keep me alive.

After he shoots Avery with the tranq dart and she passes out cold beside me, Masked Motherfucker dresses my bullet wound silently, with more gauze and bandages from the never-ending medical kit. I'd like to say I get him into a headlock and break us out of here, but this isn't a fucking Tom Cruise movie. I've been *shot.* In a very fucking painful place. I couldn't put a kitten in a headlock right now if I tried.

After he's done playing doctor, he cuffs my wrists and ankles, throws a bag over my head, and drags me out of the room by my feet.

I fight him as much as I can, but every time I jerk

around, I feel more blood spurt up out of my bullet wound. A few ill-placed kicks that barely hit the asshole, and I'm almost dead with blood loss.

I decide to stop fighting and play dead instead. Or, at least, play unconscious. At least if this guy is dragging me out of here, an almost-corpse for him to dispose of, he can't hurt Avery. I mentally catalog everything as I drag along the ground; from the rough concrete floor of our dungeon for two, to another room, the one that's behind the one-way glass, where I presume this sick fuck has been watching over Avery with his dick in his hand. The floor in here is carpeted, soft. It smells like fresh paint, and I wonder what kind of person paints a room with a fresh coat of paint in preparation to turn it into a viewing platform for their own personal torture chamber. I mean, what kind of fucking color swatches does one pick up from the Hardware store for such a room? Did he go straight to the reds, or has he chosen a more ironic shade?

I hear more locks, more doors. My head bounces on something hard, maybe a brick, and then over damp grass. I'm outside. I hear the rustling of trees, the thunk of a key turning inside a metal barrel, and then, before I know what's happening, I'm thrown into what I think is the trunk of a car.

I feel someone close to my head as I lay awkwardly on plastic sheeting. Great. This is the part where I get wrapped up with a bunch of bricks and thrown off the Golden Gate Bridge. I hold my breath, squeezing my eyes tight, waiting for the split second of recognition that a bullet has been fired into my skull. It never comes, though, just a distorted voice in my ear, a threat uttered through the calico bag over my head. "Try anything, and I will gut her and make you wear her skin."

I very much doubt I would fit into Avery Capulet's skin, her narrow frame no match for my bulk, but that's not the message contained in the threat, is it? No. I imagine her being splayed open as punishment for my disobedience, and part of me dies, a part I didn't know was still buried underneath all of the festering hate I have for the Capulets. The trunk slams shut, and despite every cell in my body screaming to attempt some kind of escape, I don't try a damn thing.

I pass in and out of consciousness as we drive, straining to hear anything outside that might indicate where we are. At one point I think we might be on the Golden Gate Bridge, but I can't be sure. It could be the Bay Bridge. It could be the goddamn surface of Mars.

Eventually, we come to a stop, the trunk is cracked open, and I'm lifted from one car to another. Something stabs into my arm, and I don't wake up again or what feels like a very, very long time.

When I do rouse again, it's so fucking bright, I assume I've died. I'm on my back, cold steel underneath me. Am I dead? Is this my autopsy? Jesus Fuck, am I trapped in my own dead body?

"Is this hell?" I mutter.

A deep voice sounds beside me. "Probably."

I blink rapidly, trying to get my bearings. It's so damn bright. I can vaguely make out two heads, faces wrapped in surgical masks. As my vision clears, I look from one side to the other, of what must be a metal gurney I'm laying on. Two dudes, both black, both tall, performing surgery on me, without any goddamn anesthetic, judging by the pain in my shoulder. I try to gauge if I recognize them, taking in their features as best I can with my screwed-up vision. One is slightly taller, his head shaved, dark eyes the only thing I can see above his blue surgical mask. The other one, digging around in my fucking shoulder, has dark hair, cut close to his skull. As soon as I see them, I have my suspicions about who they are. But I don't say anything.

"Some drugs wouldn't hurt," I say, coughing.

"Since you're digging around in my fucking shoulder."

One of the guys leans over to address me. "You've got enough downers in your system to kill a horse," he says. "I give you any more, you're gonna die right here."

Well, at least that confirms that I'm not already dead.

"This is gonna hurt," he warns, placing a mouthguard in between my teeth. "Bite on this if you need."

Great. With a giant piece of rubber in my mouth rendering me mute, I feel this dude slice into my shoulder. I roar around the mouthguard, the pain white-hot, and then I pass the fuck out.

The pain is still there as I slip under a shallow sort of unconsciousness, but it's slightly dulled. A self-protective coping mechanism the body provides, I suppose. I dream while the bullet is dug out of my body.

I dream of Avery Capulet.

---

*S*he was leaning against the back wall of horse stables at the spot where our properties met the first time I saw her smoking. Alone, her *dark wavy hair stacked on top of her head in a messy topknot, dressed in cutoff denim shorts and an old Metallica t-shirt. Clothes too plain for a rich girl like her, but they suited her perfectly. Made her look less prissy bitch and more ordinary fifteen-year-old girl. Though, there was nothing ordinary about Avery Capulet. Even dressed in rags, she'd be more beautiful than any girl in Verona, and beyond.*

I was standing in my kitchen; or, what used to be a kitchen, when I noticed her. I hadn't been back to the house in a long time, not in the years since the place had burned down, my brother perishing in the fire before my mother could get him out. Now, I was here to meet a bank assessor, part of the conditions of my trust fund that controlled the property. The single crown in the destroyed Montague crown that had been left unsold. Because the house and its surrounding property, much to the ire of Avery's father, was mine, and I wasn't letting it go without a fight. The house itself had been long since condemned; the Town of Verona kept insisting it was a danger that needed to be sold off and razed to the ground.

There was only one way the Capulets were taking the last thing my family had to their name — from my cold, dead hands. And I didn't intend on dying any time soon.

I was almost eighteen. Almost an adult. And the moment the house left the security of my trust fund and became mine to do with as I saw fit, I knew they'd circle like vultures, looking to dismantle the property and force a sale. To them.

I'd never sell it to them. I'd sooner burn down their house than let them have what was left of mine.

Avery Capulet. I saw her, alright, without the protection of a thick woolen skirt and long-sleeved cotton to cover her up. All the blood in my body rushed to my dick when I saw her like that, one knee bent so her foot rested on the wall. She saw me, too, across the overgrown orchards and waist-high grass that flanked my giant, fire-damaged eyesore that loomed from the earth like an open wound. The bank assessor in my kitchen kept talking away, but I stopped hearing his words. All I saw was Avery Capulet, looking exactly as I'd imagined her dressed in something other than the navy tartan knee-length skirts and pressed white shirts that formed the girls uniform at our school.

She looked like a lamb to a lion like me. And I'll admit: my mouth watered at the thought of biting into her pale flesh and leaving a mark.

I cut off the bank assessor abruptly, signed the forms he needed to keep my house in trust until the new set of obligations had been fulfilled, and ushered him out of my house as quickly as possible. The moment he exited the rusted gates that led to the street, I made a beeline for the boundary fence that separated the Capulet property from mine. The wall was impressive, except for the fact that there were holes in it, probably cut by Avery and her sister to sneak out without Daddy knowing.

If Avery saw me approaching, she didn't react. She just kept her shiny brown eyes leveled at the empty pool behind my house, the spot where snakes liked to explore and mosquitoes laid their eggs. I pulled a hole in the wire fencing apart wide enough to step through, and then I was right in front of this strange girl I'd once been supposed to marry.

"Those things'll kill you," I said, puncturing the silence. Avery just smiled, a secret smile that I would eventually learn was only for me. She took a drag of the cigarette, taking a step closer to the invisible line that ran between us. She tilted her head up, a foot shorter than me, and breathed out a cloud of smoke that made my eyes water. Slender fingers offered me the half-smoked Marlboro with a smirk. "You wanna die with me?"

Her words were a dare. Maybe, even then, they were a premonition of our future. But to my ears, they were just smartass words from a pretty girl's mouth. A girl I had no business being near, much less trespassing on her property.

I looked at her mouth as she waited for my response, glossy lips in a perfect rosebud shape. I imagined what it might be like to kiss a girl like Avery Capulet, and the thought made my mind go to dark places, to flashes of pink nipples and insistent tongues.

I took the cigarette and put it between my lips, sucking the toxic shit into my lungs. The burn wasn't entirely unpleasant. That was my first mistake.

I tasted her cherry lipgloss on the stub of the cigarette, and I was a fucking goner.

"Selling?" Avery asked, gesturing to the bank assessor who was still at the front of my property, talking on his cellphone. The edge of my mouth curled up in a smirk.

"I bet your father would like that."

Avery shrugged, taking another drag of her cigarette. "Of course he would. He has to look at it every day. I'm sure he'd prefer it bulldozed."

"Mmm," I replied, raking my eyes up and down her legs. Fuck, she wasn't that tall, but somehow, her

fawn-like legs went forever. I licked my lips again, tasting that cherry gloss, laughing inwardly at the irony.

"What's so funny?" Avery asked.

"Oh, nothing. I was just thinking of what old Augie's going to say when he realizes he can't buy my house. Ever. Not unless I get married, that is. Until then, that piece of shit is untouchable."

She tilted her head to the side, looking me up and down the same way I'd appraised her. I thought of what she must see: a piece of Montague trash, in torn-up black jeans, a t-shirt, tattoos peeking out from the bottom of my sleeves.

"Maybe I should marry you," she said dryly. "If that's what it'll take to stop my horses getting spooked by the snakes living in your garden."

I tipped my head back and laughed. "Should I get down on one knee?" I deadpanned.

I had expected a comeback. What I hadn't expected was for her to motion with a curled finger for me to lean in to her, so she could whisper something in my ear. My skin got hot in the places where my body brushed against hers, and I caught that smell of her shampoo for the first time, oranges and honey.

"I wouldn't marry you if you had the last functioning dick on earth," she said, pushing me away

with a palm to my chest. Maybe I would have been offended, but the expression on her face wasn't hateful; it was eager.

"The last functioning dick, huh?" I echoed, plucking the almost-finished cigarette from her fingers and taking the last puff. I blew the smoke back in her pretty face, and she didn't even flinch. I stepped closer to her, caging her against the wall with my arms. "I don't need a dick to make you scream, Avery Capulet. I've got a tongue, and two hands, and I wouldn't need to marry you to make you come on either of those things."

Blood rushed to her cheeks when I said that. I smirked, dropping the cigarette butt on the ground and crushing it beneath my sneaker. I turned and walked away, feeling her eyes as they burned into the back of me, both of us knowing that I had won this time.

CHAPTER EIGHTEEN

ROME

*N*obody ever paid attention to us when we were young. She was second-in-line for a throne that her older sister had already been molded to fit. I was the ruins of a family legacy that had soared too high, and crashed spectacularly, the sole survivor of a broken dynasty.

We were both afterthoughts to our fathers; mine, who had been driven out of town after the fire; and hers, who was focused only on Adeline, the oldest Capulet offspring, the prodigal daughter who would ascend the throne.

But *I* paid attention to Avery Capulet. And she paid attention to me. And something about the fact that we were forbidden only made me want her more.

Love isn't always a happy thing.

Sometimes it's a dirty habit, a vice that makes you miserable with need. A desperate addiction that threatens to kill you in every moment that you spend apart. There's no happiness in love when you know it has an expiration date. Only an anxious, gnawing grief of a future you both already know, a day when you'll be forced apart. Avery and I knew our time was finite. Our story's ending was hurtling toward us at the speed of light. We just thought we had more time.

And then Avery's sister died, and our end arrived quietly, like a snake, sinking its poison into us before we knew we'd been bitten. Even as I was breathing air into Adeline Capulet's water-filled lungs, pumping her chest with my flattened palms hard enough to feel her ribs crack under the force, I knew I had lost Avery. Like a thief, death stole more than just Adeline from her family, and from my best friend, who truly loved her; death stole the future we'd all hoped could somehow one day be a reality.

Loving Avery Capulet didn't make me happy. It made me heartsick. So when she betrayed me, it was the worst pain I'd ever endured; but it was also, in some strange way, a relief.

he next time I wake up, I wonder if it was all a dream. The two guys who operated on me. The car journey. The guy who raped Avery. Was it all just some fucked up nightmare?

Avery's face swims in my vision. I'm back on the mattress, the cuffs gone, the bullet out of my shoulder, leaving a biting pain in its wake. I blink once, twice, my eyes focusing enough to see the look on Avery's face, and I know none of it was fictional. It was a nightmare, yes, but not the kind you wake up from.

"Where did you go?" she whispers. "Where did he take you?"

I shrug, still trapped halfway between sleep and wake. "A little trip to the surgeon," I mutter. "For someone who's going to brutally murder us, he sure did seem to want me alive."

Which is extremely fucking troubling. A killer who has underground surgeons save his victims. Who he shot. I can't make it add up.

"I thought you were dead," Avery whispers. She has new clothes on, a white t-shirt and a black skirt that ends mid-thigh; and she's clean, no longer covered in our blood. She's even wearing some kind of necklace, a thick black choker that looks like it's made of leathery plastic.

"One little bullet isn't going to kill a Montague," I murmur. Avery smiles at that. And then immediately bursts into tears.

"I'm sorry," she whispers. "I'm sorry, I'm sorry, I'm sorry."

"Why?" I reply, a little too bitterly. "*You* didn't shoot me."

I ty to sit up, groaning at the flash of red-hot agony that sparks across my shoulder and through my body when I move. *Motherfucker.* Getting shot is so fucking inconvenient. Give me a good stabbing any day.

Avery moves to help me, and that makes me angry.

I shrug off her assistance, watching the hope on her face fade to resignation as she sits back on her heels. With difficulty, I eventually maneuver myself into a sitting position against the wall. I look down at myself, confused when I see I'm wearing a new black t-shirt, dark denim jeans. These aren't my clothes. I look Avery up and down again, taking in her new clothes, her clean hair. "Did you go to the mall or something while I was gone?"

Her eyes blank for a second. Her face falls, her

hand coming up to finger the choker she's wearing around her neck. Suspicion peaks in my chest immediately; I know where I've seen one of those before. It's not a necklace. It's a fucking collar.

A collar you would put on a *dog*.

"What is that?" I ask, alarm bells ringing underneath the pain. I'm talking barely above a whisper, trying to speak without being heard by whoever is outside the room, watching us, but they can probably hear every word I say. Between the one-way glass and the cameras, I doubt I can think in this room without being heard.

Her amber-colored eyes, the same eyes I remember always being full of fire, are blank now, shiny with unshed tears. She looks so bereft, it's almost frightening. And I don't scare easy. But when it comes to Avery, I've never been able to regulate any kind of emotion. Raging lust. Forbidden love. Fierce loyalty. And then, the thing that replaced it all. Hate. Black, festering, hate.

My soul might have died every time I thought about her after she fucked me over, until I was hollowed out of anything good and filled with bitter hatred, but I can't hate the girl sitting in front of me with a collar around her neck. She's too pained, too damaged.

Love makes you weak, my father said to me once, after my brother died. *Hate keeps you strong.* He was referring to the Capulets, of course, the engineers of our ruin.

Love. Makes. You. Weak.

I can't afford to be weak, not if we're going to get out of here alive.

Don't feel sorry for her, I tell myself. *She destroyed you once. If you let her, she'll destroy you all over again.*

She still hasn't answered me.

"Avery!" I hiss. "What happened while I was gone?"

Big, fat tears roll down her face as she shakes her head emphatically. She can't even talk about what happened, yet she knows exactly what I saw. Was it worse? How could it get any worse?

She opens her mouth as if to speak when there's a loud crash from the other side of the one-way glass. Both of us freeze, her overflow of emotion turned off like a faucet, my pain forgotten as fresh dread lances through my weary bones. I'm not about to be on the ground when this psycho comes back in, so I stand as quickly as I can, bracing my good arm against the wall as I get to my feet. Everything spins for a second, so I blink until the sensation of falling goes away.

Avery is next to me, her hands clutching at that collar around her throat. I've seen something like it before, but I can't place it. Instinctively, using my non-shot arm, I press Avery behind me slightly, positioning my body so he has to get through me to get to her. I mean, I'm sure a small child could push me over right now, what with the being shot and all, but I've at least got to put up a fight.

Avery starts to shake behind me as the heavy metal door swings open, the man from before still dressed exactly the same, in his all black attire and matching black balaclava. He's got a gun in one hand, a knife in the other, and it pisses me the fuck off that I've got nothing to defend us with except my one good arm. I mean, the guy's wearing steel-capped boots, and I don't even have a pair of shoes.

The guy comes closer, brandishing the large butcher's knife in Avery's direction. I keep tucking her behind me, following the guy as he circles us in this narrow space, a weapon in each hand. And suddenly, her betrayal falls away. It doesn't matter what she did; only that I loved her, once. It only matters that the part of me that once burned for her is still there, hidden under all the anger and the hurt. I still love her.

And the thought of this guy hurting her, the ways he's already hurt her; I can't bear it. I've been this terrified exactly once before. When I woke up, just a kid, and my entire bedroom was on fire. I got out. My brother didn't. He burned to death while concerned neighbors held my mother so she wouldn't run back inside and burn too.

I am that scared now. Terrified of what all this might mean. Sick to my stomach at the prospect of having to watch Avery be violated again.

"Hurt me," I say. "Don't hurt her."

The guy stops, his head tilting slightly, and I hear a muffled laugh. He holds the knife out to me, and I reach my fingers out on pure instinct, willing to risk grabbing the knife when it's this close to me, even though it's probably a trap.

"I'm not going to hurt her," he says in that distorted voice, pressing the handle of the knife into my open palm.

"You are."

THANK YOU SO MUCH FOR READING
VICIOUS PRINCE

Rome and Avery's story continues in

VENGEFUL QUEEN

Sign up for my newsletter to find out about my upcoming releases: www. lilisaintgermain.com/newsletter

ABOUT THE AUTHOR

Lili St. Germain is a *USA Today* bestselling hybrid author who writes books about vengeful girls, villainous men, and forbidden love.

Her books have sold over a million copies worldwide since January 2014.

The **Gypsy Brothers** series focuses on a morally bankrupt biker gang and the girl who seeks her vengeance upon them. The **Cartel** series is a prequel trilogy of full-length novels that explores the beginnings of the club and the drug kingpin who dictates their every move.

Aside from writing, her other loves in life include her gorgeous husband and beautiful daughter, good coffee, Tarantino movies and spending hours on Instagram.

She loves to read almost as much as she loves to write.

Made in the USA
Monee, IL
05 April 2021